I0632794

CLOSE UP

LOVE, CAMERA, ACTION #3

ELISE FABER

Elise Faber
SNARKY BOOKS FOR SNARKY MINDS

CLOSE UP
BY ELISE FABER

This is a work of fiction. Names, places, characters, and events are fictitious in every regard. Any similarities to actual events and persons, living or dead, are purely coincidental. Any trademarks, service marks, product names, or named features are assumed to be the property of their respective owners, and are used only for reference. There is no implied endorsement if any of these terms are used. Except for review purposes, the reproduction of this book in whole or part, electronically or mechanically, constitutes a copyright violation.

CLOSE UP
Copyright © 2020 Elise Faber
Print ISBN-13: 978-1-63749-014-3
Ebook ISBN-13: 978-1-946140-57-9
Cover Art by Jena Brignola

LOVE, CAMERA, ACTION

Dotted Line

Action Shot

Close Up

End Scene

ONE

Eden

I WALKED out of the hospital after visiting Artie and Pierce's beautiful baby girl, my heart filled with so much joy for my friends.

I owed the director-producer duo a huge debt of gratitude.

They'd cast me in the surprise box office success, *Carrot*, a few years before, and because of that, I'd had my dream of crossing over from model to actress fulfilled. I'd been one of those model urban legends, a pretty girl seen on the street and approached, my career in modeling easy and fruitful. I hadn't been taken in by a creepy old man with a casting couch nor had I been assaulted or belittled or had a diary filled with horror stories like so many of my contemporaries.

I was lucky.

I was *empty*.

Because of everything that had happened before I'd been "discovered."

But my past had meant that I'd learned, become smarter.

And though I'd eventually managed to escape, I was left a shell of a person because of it.

Merely a doll to be dressed up and styled in someone else's vision, a simple vessel to be filled with someone else's ideas. I was to be looked at and not looked *in*—

I snorted. It wasn't like acting was so different. I continued to be judged by the way I looked. Magazines still frequently accused me of being pregnant after I'd had a big lunch, or linked me with any male I was seen exchanging a few words with.

But I wasn't empty any longer.

I felt and lived and finally was *me*.

So much self-contemplation for so early in the morning, but then again, seeing a precious little bundle of life brought so newly into this world would do that to a girl.

I was absolutely thrilled for Artie and Pierce. They were the real deal and deserved every bit of their success—film or family version. Smiling to myself, I reached into my purse for my keys then promptly dropped them to the ground.

Ugh.

I bent—

"I know that ass."

A gasp of outrage on my lips, I straightened and whipped around, ready to tell off the arrogant bastard who'd dared—

Damon Garcia.

Photographer extraordinaire and—

He grinned.

Man who still wanted to get into my pants.

Now, I wasn't a prude. I slept around enough to have been called a whore by more than one publication. It wasn't like my activities between the sheets were more than most men in Hollywood, but because I was a woman, it was noticed and frowned upon.

I just couldn't bring myself to care.

I practiced consensual, safe sex.

If we both were attracted to each other and it was safe, then I didn't hesitate to go for what I wanted.

Maybe that made me a whore.

Maybe I didn't care what other people thought about me.

But Damon?

Damon, I didn't sleep with.

Damon, I didn't fuck or kiss or touch.

Because I knew if I allowed myself a taste, I would never have enough.

I was frozen in place when he bent in front of me and picked up my keys, extending them toward me. That was when I made my first mistake. My fingers brushed his as I took them back. Heat exploded up my arm, my stomach went tingly, and my voice was breathy as I asked, "What are you doing here?"

"I live here now. Well, not the hospital—I'm visiting a friend —but here in town." He smiled, and that paired with the news of him being in L.A. hit me hard upside the head. So hard, it knocked my common sense loose and allowed me to make my second mistake.

Because I didn't run after I'd said, "Oh, that's great."

My third came when he asked, "Want to grab a drink tonight and catch up?"

To which I said, "Yes," instead of "Absolutely not."

My fourth?

Well, my fourth came when I finally gave in to the draw that was Damon Garcia and woke up naked in my bed beside him.

And then he wouldn't leave.

TWO

Eden

OH GOOD GOD. What had I done?

Damon was in my bed.

Correction. A *naked* Damon was in my bed.

I shifted carefully, slipping out of the circle of his arms and from beneath the covers, then padded quietly to the bathroom.

Let it be noted that *I* was naked, too.

Worse, it had been good. No, great. *No*, fucking incredible and the best I'd ever had.

The. Best. Ever.

I was so screwed.

After slipping into my fluffy, oversized bathrobe, I turned to stare at myself in the mirror.

"Eden Larson, you are a mess," I muttered, leaning my hands next to the sink and critically eyeing my bright red hair and pale skin. I might as well be critical because Hollywood sure wasn't going to be kind about the new wrinkles—marring my forehead—or the gray in my hair—a strip appearing just above my right ear—or my boobs—and how they'd begun to sag in recent years. I mean, look, I had a healthy appreciation for my body, and I knew I was supposed to love every inch and all of the lines and sags and wrinkles . . . but my job was predominantly based on my appearance on a giant screen or the cover of a magazine or how good I looked when I went out and was caught "unawares" by the paparazzi, and sometimes it was hard to keep perspective.

Those *Chunky Eden Has Let Herself Go* headlines didn't feel good, no matter how long I'd been in the press.

Probably why I'd given into my attraction to Damon in the first place.

The lovely gossip sheets yesterday speculating how far along I was.

Sigh.

Sometimes I hated this industry.

And the rest of the time I smacked myself out of this funk because I was really lucky to be in my position, that I'd gone from an obscure girl on a street corner approached by a model scout to one of the top models in the industry. Then, thanks to Pierce and Artie, I'd had my big break with *Carrot*.

So, there it was. I was one of the select few to successfully make the crossover from model to actor.

Go me.

That didn't change the fact that now I'd fucked the one person I'd made a promise to myself never to sleep with.

Damon Garcia was handsome and talented and funny and . . . he got me. All of which might be great things, except for the fact that getting me also meant that I had gotten attached and I couldn't afford to be. We had to go back to being just friends. We had to—

"Shit," I muttered, knowing my inner pleading was the great sex equivalent of Pandora's box. That lid was open now, and I knew all about what was inside.

Or rather, I now knew all about those hard, yummy inches and how they felt inside *me*.

Mistake. It had been a mistake.

But could something that felt as good as my night in bed with Damon really be bad?

Yes.

Of course, it was.

I'd promised myself that I wasn't going to do this. I wasn't going to get attached.

Not *ever* again.

I reached for my toothbrush and glared at myself in the mirror. "This was a mistake, Eden. You have *got* to get your shit together. Shower. Get him out of here, and then go back to your life—"

"Was it really that bad?"

I froze, Damon's voice drifting down my spine.

Fuck, I'd always loved his voice, especially when it was like that. Warm and soft, but almost predatory.

It had made my thighs clench when he'd discussed the shot list with me during our first photoshoot together all those years ago, and it still made them tense now, though the pleasure was tinged with panic.

I didn't sleep with men I liked. I couldn't afford to.

The toothbrush hit the counter with a *clink,* and I girded my loins as I spun to face him.

Not that it mattered. Despite the girding, heat still flooded my insides.

Only now it was worse.

Because I knew how good it could be.

Caramel skin, chocolate eyes, strong jaw, dark hair, and enough stubble on his cheeks to remind me with a shiver of how good that stubble had felt rubbing against my thighs.

"You need to go," I blurted.

In answer, he leaned back against the doorframe and loosely crossed his arms. "Eden, honey."

Honey down my spine.

Just like the first shoot we'd done together when he'd taken it from his assistant and poured it all over my body, dripping it this way and that until he'd gotten exactly the look he'd been going for.

The resulting photographs, me covered in the sticky stuff, glistening droplets down my skin, my body clad only in a silver bikini had, without a doubt, been the item I'd autographed the most over the years.

This will be many a teenage boy's spank bank material, Damon had teased.

He was probably right.

But he'd also made me see myself differently with that shoot.

I'd never felt sexy, or as fodder for someone's self-pleasure. I didn't doubt I was okay-looking, though more cute than sexy for sure, but those photographs had . . . well, I'd seen how I could be transformed.

And it had given me the confidence to pursue acting.

If I could transform into a sex kitten with just a silver bikini and a few jars of honey, then maybe I could transform in other ways, too. But it wasn't just being sexy, though that had definitely given me more confidence. It was that I could be seen as something more than just the superficial.

Which is why he'd also told me, *And when the important ones—the ones who can look past the bikini and honey—see this . . . well, your calendar is going to explode, sweetheart.*

He'd been right. My offers following that shoot had gotten bigger and bigger, until I'd been transformed from mid-list to one of the most well-known models in the world.

But transformations didn't help me now.

Because Damon was there and awake and . . . still naked, unabashedly leaning back against the door. It should have been kind of icky. I mean, penises weren't the most attractive body part to just be so casually on display.

But *Damon's* penis?

Yeah, I could stare at it all day.

Which I was doing. Right at that moment, watching it lengthen and harden beneath my gaze, remembering how it had felt in my mouth, how it had tasted as I'd sucked him deep, how he'd pulsed between my lips, his fingers sliding into my hair and—

Damon cleared his throat and my eyes shot to his.

His lips curved. "Morning, baby."

I whirled around, released a shaky breath. "Y-you should g-go."

Silence.

Then, "I ordered breakfast," he announced, ignoring my statement. "I hope you still like French toast." His words had gotten louder as he'd closed the distance between us, and I felt the heat of his body hit my spine. But he didn't touch me—though if I were being honest, I was almost desperate for the contact.

Fear locked my spine.

I couldn't want him.

Correction: I couldn't *still* want him.

That wasn't what I did anymore. Second dates weren't required. I didn't form lasting relationships with my lovers. One night and I was done.

And I'd never had an issue with that.

But Damon?

There was a reason I'd never slept with him before.

Fuck.

I was going around in circles and—

The doorbell rang.

My hair was swept to the side, his lips pressed to my nape. "Must be breakfast. I'll go grab it."

I locked my knees against the physical onslaught of his touch, holding back my shudder until I heard his feet pad out of the bathroom, heard the soft brush of fabric against skin that indicated him putting on his clothes, then more footfalls trailing down the hall.

Only then did I slump against the counter, resting my head in my hands.

I'd messed up.

Oh, how I'd messed up.

THREE

Damon

I'D KNOWN Eden for a long time.

I'd known I'd wanted to *sleep* with Eden for a long time.

I just hadn't expected her to let down the walls enough to make the first move. But she'd done that last night, and after only two drinks. We'd hung out enough that I knew two drinks weren't enough to get her drunk or to make it so she wasn't lucid enough to make a decision about whom she was going to sleep with.

We'd hung out a lot.

I'd watched her pick up many male hands and lead them from the bar.

Just not me. Eden had *never* chosen me.

There was a line between us, one I'd made clear I was willing to cross, one *she'd* made clear she wasn't *going* to cross.

Except, last night she'd done just that.

And now I had a bag of food in my hand, Eden was all but locked in the bathroom, and I had been given a sliver of a chance to finally get what I'd been pining after for years.

Eden.

Not just a one and done spectacular night, but Eden.

Forever.

I knew I had an uphill climb, knew that Eden was gun shy, that she didn't date or form meaningful relationships with men. Though, that wasn't an entirely fair statement. She *did* have friends—I'd been strictly in that category until last night—and she had lovers.

It was the lovers that weren't around for long.

The friends. *They* were allowed to hang.

Now I was firmly in No Man's Land.

Sighing, I debated between leaving, like Eden clearly wanted me to do, and staying, which would risk me being put back in the friends category, but would also ensure that I stayed out of the lover's section.

I didn't want to be just friends with Eden, but I liked the idea of being relegated to the periphery of her life even less.

There was a reason I'd maintained contact with her over the years, even though our connection was less important now that she'd transitioned over to films and I'd remained firmly in photography.

I didn't have any desire to enter Hollywood or to direct films or TV, like some of my colleagues. I was happy to shoot a portrait of a star or fashion or bikini shots (Eden's, in particular, had shifted my focus, that was for damn sure). But what all of those had in common was good money *and* exposure. And yet . . . they didn't feed my soul, and for the most part, they weren't particularly interesting. I couldn't say that as a be-all-end-all because there were often undertones and interesting personalities beneath the veneer of celebrities, but it was typically a struggle to have the time and patience to reveal them.

Still, those shoots were important because they padded my

bank account, kept me busy and in the right circles, and gave me freedom.

The freedom to pursue the subjects that did feed my soul.

Some might call those subjects nobodies, but those so-called nobodies were so much more open than a PR-represented, agented celebrity. Or if they *weren't* open, they usually had more time in front of the lens to peel back the layers.

Eden hadn't fit into either of those categories when I'd first met her.

She'd been a successful model, not world-renowned like after the photographs had hit, but those photos had also catapulted *me* onto a whole other tier along with her. Still, while she'd been in the industry and knew how shoots worked and what was expected, she'd also been . . . open.

Her pain, her vulnerability, her insecurities had shown through her eyes, had bled right over into the photographs.

And it had transformed that silver bikini and honey photo—as we'd been ordered to undertake by the male magazine, neither of us having the clout or funds to turn down such a big job—from just sexy and superficial into something more.

More because it wasn't just teenage boys who'd love it (though they definitely had). More because it was also appreciated by housewives and feminists.

Because it wasn't just sex.

It was more.

Just like she was.

Sighing, I set the bag on Eden's kitchen table and began unpacking the contents. She might not think she was worth more than just sex, but I knew differently. She deserved to be seen for all those things that were present in the photo—vulnerable, but strong; insecure, but pushing through; sexy, but because she was finding it for herself.

Eden was all of those things.

So, I wasn't giving up on her.

Nope. She'd opened the door. Perhaps it was just barely ajar, but I was going to shove my foot into that gap, and I was going to *keep* nudging it open, until that sliver was pushed wide.

I was in.

I wasn't going anywhere.

Soft footsteps down the hall told me that she was approaching, but I pretended not to hear, just continued unpacking the food, opening the containers, setting the silverware on napkins next to them.

Only then did I turn and smile at her. "Hey, sweetheart."

Green eyes went wide, lush pink lips parted. "I— You . . . sh-should—"

I plunked my ass into the seat and started eating the omelet I'd ordered.

Silence.

"Come and eat," I said around a mouthful of eggs, bacon, and cheese. "Before it gets cold."

My gaze flicked up, saw she hadn't moved.

Stubborn.

I forced my lips not to curve up then reached for her food. "Oh? Not hungry? I'll just have to eat this French toast—"

She crossed the room quickly, tugging the takeout box from my hands and glaring at me. "Mine," she muttered and lifted it up, inhaling deeply and releasing a soft moan that had my cock twitching.

I'd heard that moan plenty the night before.

Her eyes shot to mine. "Damon—"

"Sit," I ordered. "Eat."

It was almost comical, watching the debate on her face, her desire to put distance between us, to shove me away, warring with her need for sugar-covered carbs.

Thankfully, after knowing her for so long, I understood her weaknesses.

And sugar was one.

Breakfast foods were the other—in particular order, French toast, waffles with strawberries and cream, and blueberry pancakes. The rest were good, but carbs were where it was at—and I was quoting her directly here.

Eventually, she sat . . . in the chair the absolute furthest away from me.

No matter.

I stood, grabbed my food, and brought it to the one next to hers, half-surprised when she didn't stand and move in turn, spurring us into a leapfrog of chairs and takeout containers.

I was game.

She was more mature.

She just sighed softly, picked up her fork, and started eating.

Another moan, another cock twitch. And really, my cock shouldn't be capable of twitching. It should be completely out of commission after the previous eighteen hours. I'd come four times, trying to make the most of my time, trying to orgasm the fear and distance out of Eden.

Based on our little dance right now, I hadn't succeeded.

Though, I did take a little comfort in the fact that she *was* uncomfortable. Probably made me a dick, but discomfort was at least an emotion.

It wasn't cutting me off or shutting me out completely.

That little sliver was still open.

I could still keep pressing forward.

"Here," I murmured, picking up a container of syrup and opening it for her when she seemed to be looking around for one.

Eden froze then reached out and took it from me, careful to keep our fingers from brushing.

No matter. *That* was something, too.

Not distant. Not unaffected.

I waited until she had a bite of her breakfast an inch from her lips before asking, "So, was I that bad of a fuck?"

She inhaled rapidly, sucking in a puff of powdered sugar then immediately began coughing. *Fuck.* Reaching over, I patted her back. The wrong thing to do in this situation—the patting, and in fairness, probably the words, too. I'd been trying to shock her. On the other hand, I wasn't trying to *kill* her.

"Arms up," I said, taking the fork from her hand and setting it in the container, helping her lift them overhead. My sister, Cindy, who was an EMT, had taught me that trick, and it worked by allowing a bit more air into the lungs, though it wouldn't do anything if Eden was actually choking.

Thankfully, in this case, it was just a short burst of coughing.

Then she was able to suck in a deep breath and reach for her napkin.

She wiped her lips, slowed her breathing. I popped up, searched her cabinets until I'd found a glass and filled it with water, then brought it back to her.

"Thanks," she croaked, taking it and guzzling down a long sip.

I smiled and it was chagrined. "Sorry for nearly killing you."

Green eyes flicked to mine, narrowed.

"Not sorry for last night though."

Alarm swept across her face. "Dam—"

"Carbs," I interrupted. "Eat them."

She glanced from the food to me. "I—"

"Sugar and syrup and carby deliciousness," I coaxed.

A sigh, but she picked up her fork and started shoveling food into her mouth. I abandoned my omelet and started in on the potatoes before getting up and pouring myself a glass of water. Then I sat down next to Eden and watched her polish off an almost obscenely large amount of French toast without skipping a beat.

She kept her eyes down and pounded that food like a soldier hurrying through chow time. Efficient, quick, impressive.

But then again, Eden did love her carbs.

And probably also loved avoiding just this kind of interaction that I'd engineered. Tough. She was going to have to deal with me. I could match her in stubbornness and she liked me, I knew it—

You're delusional, bro.

Why was it that every time I had an inner thought that wasn't positive, it came in the sound of my sister's voice?

Probably because Colleen was . . . persistent.

Well, fine. I didn't have much choice if Eden really did kick me out, but I did have an opportunity in front of me, one that could prove to her we were good together. People weren't friends for six years without building trust and a rapport, and people certainly didn't have as much chemistry between the sheets as we'd had without exploring it more than once.

Well, more than one night anyway.

Plus, I liked Eden. She was beautiful, of course, but she was also smart and witty, had a generous heart, and was kind.

Those characteristics didn't tend to hang around for long in Hollywood.

But success hadn't changed her.

"So, did you get the final script?"

Eden and I had been having weekly calls since the picture had hit all those years before. I'd called to check on her, made sure she was fine, and then we'd kept in touch, talking or Face-Timing every Thursday night at eight P.M., Pacific time.

Those calls meant that I knew she had a full year of shooting and promotion in front of her.

A rom-com called *Her Point of View,* followed by an action flick named *Born Free,* then later that fall a few weeks shooting a small part Pierce Daniels had given her in his latest superhero film, and then promotion for several projects from last year slotted in between.

These weeks in L.A. were her last free ones for a while.

And she was going to spend most of it learning lines, prepping for time away, and relaxing before being pulled in a million different directions.

Being the lead in the rom-com and action film meant that a lot of pressure would be resting on her shoulders and her ability to draw in an audience. I knew that she was worried about it, along with worried about being prepared for *Her Point of View* when she'd received word that some scenes had been reworked.

Her eyes drifted to mine and stayed.

I smiled. "Think of it like our weekly call. I want to catch up with you."

Softness invading her expression, a smile curling the edges of her lips. "I do like having a standing appointment to complain about everything in my life."

"You hardly complain," I began.

"The wrong kind of chocolate in my dressing room?" she asked, lips twitching. "My male costar getting handsy?"

Red flared behind my eyes, and I almost wished she hadn't brought that particular memory up. I'd given her a little advice on pressure points and how to execute a knee to the groin.

She relaxed and laughed. "Your face." Her hand covered mine, fingertips slightly sticky from the powdered sugar, and I couldn't help but remember the moment I'd first fallen for her . . . approximately two seconds after dripping that honey down her porcelain skin.

Pervert? Yes, I was.

But also, appreciative of a woman who could dive into something without hesitation? Yes, that, too, and I wasn't dumb enough to not realize *that* was way more valuable than external beauty.

"I was fine," she said. "It took one *accidental* knee to get him to keep his distance, and then your recommendation of an Intimacy Coordinator in my contract moving forward was brilliant."

I flipped my palm, laced our fingers together. "I'm glad I could help."

She studied me. "You still want to murder the bastard though, don't you?"

"Yup."

A squeeze of our hands before she pulled away and picked her fork up again. "Thanks for breakfast," she murmured.

"I—"

She leaned forward, robe gaping and affording me a glimpse of creamy skin and untethered breasts.

My cock twitched again.

Hell, that was a lie.

It went rock-hard, especially when she bent further and scooped up a drip of syrup from the edge of the box, bringing it to her mouth and sucking it off.

Fuck.

The anger edging my vision from the memories of that asshole putting his hands on Eden faded and was replaced with heat. It burned through me, made me impulsive, loosened my tongue and—

"I'd buy you breakfast every day if it meant watching you lick that powdered sugar off your lips."

She froze, pointer finger sucked partway into her mouth.

All I could think was how much I wanted my cock there instead.

FOUR

Eden

I WAS LOCKED IN PLACE, the molten chocolate of Damon's eyes locked on mine.

God, he was pretty.

And funny and amazing and sexy and—

My pussy clenched.

I wanted him again. Despite my rules, despite my stupidity in acting on the attraction between us in the first place.

I'd . . . been weak.

But I'd been emotional, touched by the love I'd witnessed between Pierce and Artie when they'd held their newborn baby, wishful that I might find someone who could love me that way, but also knowing that it was impossible.

To be loved as deeply as that, I would have to open myself up.

And . . . I couldn't.

I'd done that once, thrown all caution to the wind, loved wholly and deeply and with every fiber of my being, and it hadn't meant anything in the end. Not one fucking thing, aside from the fact that it had nearly broken me.

So no, I couldn't do that again.

Hence the one-time rule.

But—

I slowly slid my finger from between my lips and set my hands in my lap.

"Damon," I whispered.

God, how I liked him. God, how I wanted him.

His eyes dipped down, and my gaze followed it, saw that my robe had opened, revealing a good amount of cleavage. I was a bit more well endowed when compared to model standards and tended to carry my extra weight there.

Damon hadn't seemed to mind last night.

Heat at the memory, arrowing through my stomach, pebbling my nipples, and making me ache. Why hadn't I just put on clothes? I should have gotten completely dressed, not left skin visible and been naked under the robe—

It wouldn't have mattered.

I could be wearing a full suit of armor and I'd still want him.

That hadn't changed over six years, over thousands of miles. The moment I heard his voice, saw his face, smelled his scent, I went wet.

His eyes came back up, still hot, still taking my breath away.

He reached toward me and I stifled a shiver in anticipation, already primed to feel those roughened fingertips trailing down my skin. But instead of brushing my chest, instead of reaching beneath my robe to cup one of my breasts, he lightly tugged the material closed.

I'd buy you breakfast every day if it meant watching you lick that powdered sugar off your lips.

The words, the heat, the not assuming I'd simply fall in his lap just because he'd said something that had made my pussy wet . . . all contributed to making me do what I did next.

Which was dropping my fork.

"Ed—"

I pushed back my chair.

"—en—"

I straddled his lap.

He gaped up at me.

I dropped my mouth to his.

Nothing, but only for a heartbeat, and then he was moving, arms banding around my waist, lips moving against mine, tongue thrusting home as he took control of the kiss. There wasn't any tentativeness or time wasted trying to learn each other's preferences. We'd done that all last night.

This was diving straight into the deep end, tongues tangling, my teeth nipping on his bottom lip and loving the way it made him growl, him lacing his fingers in my hair and gripping tightly enough to just sting the slightest . . . exactly how I liked it.

He stood and kicked back his chair, my legs still wrapped around his hips, my body all but a barnacle as I clung to him.

I thought he'd stride down the hall, dump me on the bed.

Instead, he leaned forward and set me on the table, tugging my arms and legs free from his body and then opening the robe and spreading me like I was his favorite meal.

Distantly, I heard the boxes and silverware hit the floor, the *glug* of a glass overturning and water dripping from the table and onto the tile. But that was *very* distantly because I'd propped myself up on my elbows and was much more focused on Damon.

On his scalding gaze.

On the fact that he'd dropped to his knees.

On him bending forward and his mouth pressing to my pussy.

Even knowing it was coming, I still gasped at the first touch of his tongue. Then my elbows gave way and I slumped back onto the table. He wasn't slow or gentle or coaxing.

He demanded.

And I was happy to oblige.

My hands dropped to my sides, nails trying and failing to find purchase on the wood as he worked me with his tongue. Long, slow strokes were interspersed with short, quick flicks against my clit. He sucked at my labia, used a finger to press inside. In seconds, my nerves were firing, heat and moisture and desire spiraling up and out of control. He used the flat of his tongue then the tip, alternating the movements, twisting that pleasure higher and higher as he slid his finger in and out, in and out.

Haze filled my vision, my hips bucked, my spine arched against the table. My orgasm was there, so fucking close that I could almost reach out and touch it and—

"Damon!" I shouted, fingers gripping his head and almost tearing at his hair as I tugged him back.

He stopped, leaned away, chest heaving, face severe, eyes burning.

"Inside me," I gasped, tugging him up. He was already on his feet by the time I finished the request, knocking my hands away effortlessly, fingers reaching for the button of his jeans.

"Eden?" he asked, pausing there, hands trembling.

I sat up, undid the button, tugged down the zipper.

He pushed them down. "Baby?"

I nodded.

One stroke filled me.

I didn't think about protection. I should have, but I didn't.

Instead, I just felt. His hard cock inside me, the table beneath me, the pleasure spiraling in my stomach, making my head spine. The way he looked at me and how it made my heart skip a beat, the way his hand found my hip, fingers opening and closing as though I were making him slowly lose control.

And maybe I was.

Because he'd definitely done the same to me.

My hips met his stroke for stroke, my fingers clenched his forearms, my pussy squeezed the hard intrusion of his cock.

Over and over, higher and higher. Until . . .

Thank fuck.

I catapulted over the edge.

One stroke. Another. And Damon's forehead dropped to my shoulder as he came with a long, deep groan.

I closed my eyes.

Pleasure had deadened my limbs, made my mind fuzzy. But not for long. Pretty soon reality began to creep back in, fear licking at my fingertips, eating away at the lovely after effects.

Fuck.

I'd never be able to eat at this table again.

In for a penny.

I didn't protest when Damon lifted me from the table and carried me down the hall and into the bathroom. Nor did I protest when he turned on the shower, stripped his clothes and my robe away, then put us both under the hot spray.

I didn't protest as he washed my body, nor as he dried me off afterward and brushed my hair.

I didn't protest when he tucked me under the covers and then went back into the hall.

I just listened to his footsteps enter the kitchen, listened as he cleaned up the mess we'd made there.

I should have helped.

I didn't.

Instead, I just lay there, trying to figure out how to fix this.

I couldn't fix this. I didn't know how.

The last time I hadn't kept my interactions to one night had ended up with me wearing a ring on my left hand and a cast on my other.

The last time had taken my independence.

The last time had broken me.

"Shit," I muttered, tears welling in my eyes, terror making my heart skip a beat. I needed to get out of bed, get dressed, and make sure Damon left.

And yet, I just continued to lie there. Paralyzed, weak, fucking stupid as hell. All I could think of was *his* face, the dark slashes of brows drawing together, the hand lifting before it made contact with my face. The need to layer on extra foundation for days. The way I'd had to move cautiously and carefully because he'd also struck my ribs repeatedly.

No.

No.

I was never going to be that person again.

I was strong. I was independent. I was—

Damon walked back into the room, a dish towel tossed over one shoulder, carrying a plate in one hand with a sheepish smile on his face. He extended it toward me, but when I didn't move to accept it, he set it on the nightstand.

"Because I ruined the first one," he murmured. "I'm sorry it's a poor substitute." He turned and left the room again.

My eyes flicked to the plate.

Toast, though not French-style this time.

Instead he'd placed two slices of toasted bread on a plate, slathered them with butter, and covered them both in cinnamon and sugar.

And though the past faded and the angry face of my ex-husband disappeared from my mind's eye, my heartbeat didn't slow, and the terror didn't fade. Because there was a plate of toast on my nightstand and Damon had been in my kitchen making me said toast.

He'd made me toast.

He'd cooked for me because we'd fucked each other senseless on the kitchen table, knocking our breakfast to the floor in the process.

He'd tried to fix something that he'd broken.

Th-that didn't happen. It just wasn't possible—

Damon strolled back in, a glass of orange juice in one hand, a bowl in the other. Syrup. The bowl contained syrup, I realized when he set both on the nightstand.

If I was keeping things in perspective, syrup shouldn't have been my breaking point. But he'd cooked, he'd fixed, he'd brought me fucking toast and syrup. I shook my head, sitting up at the same time and tossing the covers to the side. This couldn't be happening. I couldn't *let* this happen.

I jumped up from bed, looking for . . . hell, I didn't know what. I just had to get away, and I had to do it right in that moment.

"Eden?" Damon asked, probably shocked by my whack-a-mole tendencies. "What's wrong?"

I shook my head. "I can't do this." I took a jerky step forward, starting to run . . . somewhere, but I was tugged to an abrupt halt.

Not a rough grip, not a jolting or harsh movement, but suddenly finding myself tugged to a stop, my back against a hard chest, a firm arm banded around my waist, hot breath in my ear . . . and I freaked. I didn't hear the gentle words, the soft "Baby? What is it?"

My past swarmed forward.

The darkness swamped my mind and in one heartbeat I was

back there, on the opposite coast, in that apartment with *him*, the fists and kicks coming my way and—

I snapped.

Syrup had made me snap.

"Let go of me!" I screamed and tore at Damon's arm, my nails scratching at the bare skin, creating bright red lines at first and then when he didn't let go, cutting into his flesh.

Everything happened in both fast-forward and slow motion.

I saw the first cut, watched the blood drip, drip, *drip* slowly to my gray rug.

It felt like it took an hour for that drop to hit the plush fibers.

But then it did, the crimson circle spreading, staining.

"Let go!"

The arm dropped and then time sped up, more drops hitting the carpet, stained circles of red expanding, taking over, choking me.

"Ed—"

I scuttled backward, colliding with the dresser, hearing the items on top rattle, one or two falling over with a sickening crash, the crunch of glass shattering.

"No. No," I said. "Oh God. Don't touch me. Oh God. *No*." My knees buckled, hit the hardwood on the edges of the room and I gasped out in pain.

"Shit," Damon said. "Are you okay?" He took a step toward me.

I scooted backward, hit my head against the corner of the dresser, and stifled a cry.

It was better if I was quiet.

It would be over sooner. Would stop if I was just able to stay quiet.

"Eden."

I shook my head jerkily.

"*Eden.*"

The sharp tone made me blink and probably worked better to snap me out of the past than anything else ever could. Because Damon didn't snap. Not at me. Not at anyone. Not ever.

And that his raspy, velvety voice had sharpened to a point was shocking enough to have me coming back to reality.

To painful, humiliating reality.

"Eden. Look at me." He was crouching about ten feet away, his hand clamped over his arm, blood running between his fingers. When I met his eyes, he held my gaze for a few moments then nodded, reaching over to grab the towel from where it had fallen to the floor.

Tears dripped down my cheeks, falling more steadily when I saw that I'd sliced his arm pretty badly.

"I hurt you," I whispered. "I-I'm so s-sorry."

Damon glanced up at me. "It's just a scratch."

It wasn't. And now I'd become my worst nightmare.

He stood and instinctively, I cowered back against the dresser again. He froze. "I'm not going to touch you. I'm going to back up and stand by the door until I see you didn't cut your knees or head to hell and back."

Not the softest bedside manner. In fact, it was quite terse.

But I didn't think I could handle soft and sweet at that moment.

I was critically embarrassed and ashamed and—

"Eden."

I pushed to my feet.

Silence then, "Now turn so I can make sure you're not bleeding."

I turned.

"Okay," he growled. "Your ass is back in your bed and you're eating your fucking toast."

My chin lifted, the orders piling up enough that I was starting to feel more like myself. "Stop snapping at me."

"Then eat your fucking breakfast."

"No."

"Eden."

"Fuck you, Damon."

I couldn't explain it, but for some reason, me cursing at him made Damon's shoulders relax, his face clear. "There you are, baby."

My lips parted on a surprised exhale. "What?"

"You're you again." But he didn't move from the doorway, and I couldn't lie and say I wasn't thankful. "Now, be you, but be you eating the breakfast while it's warm."

I hesitated, stomach growling, wanting to sit down and eat, but also feeling very fragile and raw and flayed open. I wanted to—

"I'll leave you alone," he murmured.

That.

I wanted to be alone. To forget I'd just done that, that I'd hurt him, that I'd freaked out and revealed—

"But I'll come back, baby. And we're going to talk about this."

Fuck.

I shook my head.

Damon didn't respond to that.

Instead, he just took a few steps back into the hall, repeated, "We're going to talk," and ordered, "Lock up when I leave." Then he turned and left.

Talk.

Fuck.

Fuck.

FIVE

Damon

I SAT in my car for several long moments, trying to figure out what had happened and trying not to feel guilty for it.

Except, I did.

Because I'd pushed.

And she'd . . .

Freaked? Yes, but that wasn't just a simple freak out, or a model throwing a hissy fit. Hell, I'd endured enough of those on set to know the difference. Which meant I knew without a doubt that hadn't been Eden pulling some drama.

That was PTSD. That was trauma. That was—

Absolute terror.

And I'd been party to it.

A drip landing on my leg had me blinking and shoving the key into the ignition. I needed to go home and deal with my arm, and *then* I needed to figure out how to move forward.

Because I had the feeling I'd just opened up a fuck-ton of painful memories, and I didn't know how I could possibly justify my pushing.

She'd asked me to leave, and I'd—

"Shit," I muttered, putting the car into reverse and backing out of the driveway, happy I'd followed her home the night before so I could leave easily now, even though me following her home had been another way for her to create distance. Run along now. Get your ass in your car and leave.

Well, *that* had worked perfectly, hadn't it?

I'd had the most spectacular sex of my life—five times over—and now . . . I might lose my friend.

The dark gloom of my emotions weighed heavily on me as I drove home. I didn't see how Eden and I could go back to normal after our night together, after this morning. I mean, clearly I'd been hoping for *abnormal*, to move in a new direction, to shove through that opening, but now I'd be a total asshole if I didn't reevaluate, at least a little bit.

What had been the trigger?

If she didn't somehow cut me completely out of her life and I could convince her to let me have a shot, would we be able to work through that trauma? Was she even capable of a relationship at all?

I'd been an egotistical ass, thinking that she just hadn't met the right man.

Meaning *me*.

I hadn't allowed a second thought as to why she didn't form meaningful relationships with the opposite sex.

Well, I sure as shit had an idea of why that was now.

My apartment was only a couple of miles away, but L.A. traffic meant that it took much longer than it should have to get there. Though at least by the time I pulled into the lot, my arm had stopped bleeding.

I had that much going for me.

Sighing, I pushed out of my car and went up to my apartment. At minimum, I'd need to clear the air with her and apologize. At maximum, I'd . . . fuck, I'd forget about that sliver of opening in the armor surrounding her heart and go back to being her friend. I'd pretend the night hadn't happened, forget about the chemistry.

Not what I wanted, but if Eden needed that, I wasn't selfish enough not to give it to her.

My place was on the third floor and mostly empty. I'd only been in L.A. for a few weeks and though I'd had a couch and bed delivered and mounted a TV to the wall, I'd basically been subsisting on DoorDash and embracing the minimalist lifestyle.

That was going to change. Or rather, the minimalist part.

Since I'd made London my home base for the last few years, I'd shipped a bunch of stuff from the U.K. I was tired of the rain and the dreary weather. I wanted sun and heat and . . . much less rain.

Plus, my family lived here. Or well, in the northern part of the state, that was, but it wasn't a long drive up, and I was looking forward to spending the few free days I had with people I was close to.

Not that I hadn't had friends or people I was close with in London, but they weren't the same as someone who'd known me my whole life. With my parents, there wasn't any pretense or B.S. or trying to be nice. And even though my sisters had scattered, Cindy in Oregon and Colleen living on the East Coast, they still regularly came home to visit.

I wanted in on that.

Plus, it was refreshing to be around my family. They called me on my shit without ill feeling and definitely didn't let asshole or egotistical behavior of any type slide. In a world where I'd become successful enough that people kissed my ass on a regular basis, I needed someone who'd be straight with me.

So, I'd moved to California to be closer to my parents, but

I'd settled in the southern portion because I didn't want to be *too* close—

Of course, there was also the fact that Eden lived here.

That hadn't factored in at all.

I snorted. Didn't even believe my own bullshit, yet alone someone else's.

After unlocking my front door, I pushed through into my nearly-empty apartment and headed to my bathroom. I thought I'd seen a first aid kit under the sink when I'd moved in. Hopefully I was right in it being there, because I sure as shit hadn't stocked up on Band-Aids during the last few weeks.

I barely had furniture, let alone an assortment of bandages.

Thankfully the kit was there, and so within a couple of minutes, I'd washed the cuts then thrown a couple of Band-Aids over them. With a wince, I left the bathroom, grabbed my laptop, and plunked my ass on the couch. I had emails to answer, meetings to schedule on my calendar, shoots coming up that I needed to prepare for, and I—

Needed a break from thinking about Eden.

That wasn't to be.

Buzz. Buzz.

I pulled my cell from my pocket.

I'm sorry I hurt you.

Hearing from Eden had been pretty much the last thing I would have *ever* predicted. I'd expected . . . what? To have to go over there and bang on her front door, demanding that we talk about what happened.

Yeah. That.

My phone vibrated again.

Damon. Are you okay?

I shook off the surprise and made my fingers move.

I'm fine. I'm more worried about you.

Silence.

I'm broken, Damon. I'm not right.

My heart squeezed.

You're not broken, baby.

A beat.

I think we both know that's not true.

Fuck, but I couldn't deny she was wrong. Or at least, not completely. She had trauma and baggage and pain that was clearly overwhelming.

I shouldn't have pushed. I'm so sorry that I didn't listen to you.

Her response came almost instantly.

Sorry that you were sweet and cooked and cleaned for me? Sorry that you gave me orgasms?

I smiled despite the circumstances.

No, not for the orgasms.

I'd never regret bringing her pleasure. It was all the rest of it that I was sorry about.

I shouldn't have grabbed you.

A beat.

*I think there were a lot of shouldn'ts that have happened
in the last twenty-four hours.*

That wasn't a lie. But I also couldn't bring myself to regret
everything about our night. Still, before I could tell her that, she
texted again.

Can we just go back to how things were before?

How could I possibly forget everything and go back to how
things were?

And yet, how could I not?

If I didn't agree and she retreated, I would lose *all* of her—
the friendship, the weekly calls, the woman I'd grown close to
over the last six years. However, if we did go back, I wouldn't
have the sex, of course, I wouldn't have the fucking spectacular .
. . well, *fucking*. But I'd also lose the connection, the freedom to
kiss and touch and stroke.

And . . . that was okay. It would suck, but what I knew deep
down was that I couldn't lose Eden. I couldn't lose my friend,
couldn't not have her in my life in some form.

Even if it wasn't the form I wanted.

Life sucked sometimes.

A man bucked up and moved on and accepted the licks
thrown his way. Then he made the best of it.

Just like I was going to.

Because Eden was worth it.

And even if I didn't get everything I'd hoped for out of our night together, I still got to keep her in my life. I still had her as a friend. I was still important enough that she'd texted first.

After everything had gone down, she'd reached out.

I could reach back.

Which was why I texted her back:

Only if you promise to give me your recipe for guacamole.

Silence. Then,

You know that's never going to happen.

I knew *a lot* of things I wanted weren't going to happen, least of all was getting my hands on her delicious dip recipe and so I sent:

Make it for me sometime?

Her reply came in a few seconds.

Sure.

But no word of when that would be, no suggestion of days and times. I had the feeling that was intentional. No, I knew Eden well enough by now to recognize it *was* intentional.

More distance.

But distance I was going to let her have.

Somewhat.

I'm still bringing pizza by tonight.

The ". . ." indicating she was typing immediately appeared, but I already had my next reply primed and ready. Because, yes, I could pull back, yes, I wouldn't pressure her for intimacy she couldn't give.

But I would be her friend.

We'll run over your lines, gorge on extra pepperoni and olives, but then I have to go home early because I'm meeting a potential tomorrow.

Lie, but I wanted to give her an out, and she didn't need to know that my plans for the following day included sitting on my ass doing absolutely nothing.

Especially when my response made the ". . ." of her response stop then start, then stop and start again.

Especially when it made her reply.

Come over at 7.

Another buzz a heartbeat later.

Don't skimp on the garlic cheese bread.

Yeah, I could give her outs and space and understanding.
But I couldn't give up on being in her life.
Even if it was only as her friend.

SIX

Eden

I WAS A COWARD.

I owed him an explanation.

I was a coward.

I—

Had pretty much been going around in circles since I'd first picked up my cell earlier that day to call him.

I was going to dial his number. I wasn't going to text but actually speak to him and explain that I'd had a horrible ex and that he'd hurt me, and I was still fucked up and broken and damaged.

And that it wasn't him.

That it was me.

It's not you, it's me.

Ugh. That sounded about as good this time around as it had all the previous times I'd gone through this loop in my brain.

So, I'd chickened out. And I'd texted instead, promising myself I'd just blurt the explanation via text and then turn off my cell.

I'd done neither.

Minimally, I'd apologized, which was the single good thing I'd done that day, but the explanation hadn't come, I hadn't been able to stop my replies, and by the end of it, Damon was coming to my house, bringing me pizza, and we were rehearsing my lines.

And then he was going home.

He'd spelled that part out clearly.

I deliberately ignored the fact that Damon leaving made a pang shoot through my heart.

I was well aware of my faults along with my past trauma and that it was influencing my present life. This wasn't me thinking I was such a bad person and didn't deserve happiness. Yes, I was damaged. Yes, there was a part of me that would never be fully healed. But I wasn't a martyr. I'd gotten through to the other side. I had friends, and I had my career. That was enough.

I was also critically aware that I would never be able to lower my guard enough to give another man power over me.

I controlled the interactions.

I said when and where and then told them to get the fuck out.

Always get the fuck out.

They just . . . none of them had ever stayed or even tried to stay.

But none of them had been Damon either. I hadn't known them well, hadn't spent years with a weekly call, dinners when we were in the same town, clubs and dancing and drinking when we'd been younger and newly successful and the most exciting thing was being allowed into the VIP section. But though that excitement—partying all night, drinking myself into oblivion—had faded after a while, my connection to Damon hadn't.

This is why I hadn't allowed myself to do this.

This is why I shouldn't have allowed myself to do it now.

Fucking biological clock and cute newborns and Artie and Pierce looking so lovingly into each other's eyes.

It had melted my brain.

I'd agreed to the drink when I'd been vulnerable, and that had stretched to a meal and more drinks and then—

Damon in my bed.

Being more spectacular of a lover than I'd ever expected. I mean, it wasn't like I hadn't hoped and prayed he would be a fantastic fuck or imagined what it would be like to have him in my bed.

But . . . he was too close.

Then last night.

Had. Been. Incredible.

And also the stupidest thing I'd ever done in my life.

Circles?

See?

Now it was 6:56 P.M. and Damon was punctual, so he would be on time. Which meant I had exactly four minutes to . .

Panic? *No.* To get my shit together? Yes. That.

"Forget the orgasms," I muttered, moving to my closet and throwing on an oversized sweatshirt. Paired with loose jeans, a tank top and T-shirt, along with white sneakers, my hair pulled back into a pony, a pink baseball cap on my head, and I was wearing as many layers of clothes as I could stand.

It was ninety degrees outside. The sun was nearly set, and my air conditioning was still going at full force. I would be roasting in all the layers, but my reasoning was sound.

Namely, if it took me forever to get undressed, then I'd be less likely to jump on top of Damon's glorious cock when he came through the door.

Didn't stop me from taking it into my mouth, though.

Eden!

I stopped, shook my head hard, glad that my inner reprimand had been in my mother's voice.

That was the surest way to douse any of my remaining desire.

Clothes, good.

Penis, bad.

Friends, good.

Anything more than friends—and that included fuck buddies—bad.

The doorbell rang.

I hurried from my closet and dashed down the hall, wanting to get as far away from my bedroom as possible. On second thought—

I ran back and shut my door.

Then turned toward the front of the house. Paused. Reconsidered.

"Shit," I muttered and hustled back, opening the door and locking it from the inside then pulling it closed. I'd have to find the key later, the one that resembled a pin but with a circle on one end that I could shove into the hole in the knob to unlock it. Otherwise, I'd be sleeping on the couch.

I nodded with approval. Worth it.

The temptation would be locked away and I—

The doorbell rang again.

"Get it together, Larsen," I muttered and got my ass to the front door. "Friends," I reminded myself. "Back to friends."

I sucked in a breath, mentally girded my chastity belt, and turned the knob.

Then was wholly unprepared for the gut punch that was Damon.

Fuck, I loved the way he looked at me, brown eyes warm, lips curled up just slightly at the edges. "Hi," he murmured and fuck, but I loved it even more when he spoke to me like that, soft and gentle and sweet. His voice was like being wrapped in a warm blanket. He held up the box. "Extra garlic bread, as requested."

All of my nervousness faded.

I nodded. "Thanks," I said and added, "Want to come in?" when he hesitated on the threshold.

"You good with this?"

Concern in those pretty chocolate eyes and I mentally chastised myself again. I'd ruined the easy rapport between us. I'd known better and I'd still—

His fingers on my cheek. "Stop it."

"I'm—"

Damon brushed by me, holding the pizza boxes aloft and stepping into the hall. I turned, saw he hadn't stopped, was disappearing into the kitchen. With a slow, deep breath, I closed the door and followed him.

He'd put slices on plates and had the blue porcelain circles in his hands by the time I made it into the room. I saw him glance toward the kitchen table then hesitate.

I deliberately avoided looking in that direction because . . . well, because orgasms and sticky syrup on my skin, the sweet smell of powdered sugar in my nose. "My . . . um . . . the script is on the coffee table in the family room if you want to eat in there."

A nod then he moved that way. "Any chance you can get me a glass of water?" he asked. "I forgot to pick up drinks."

I moved toward the fridge. "Do you want a beer?"

"That would be great. Thanks." He slipped through the doorway that led to the family room.

I was not going to make this weird. I was not. We'd forget about this morning, forget about last night, and—

"Don't forget to grab yourself one," he called.

That was enough to snap me out of my head. *Friend. Be a friend.*

"Do you want to run through the full script?" he asked when I came through with a beer in each hand, "or just the rewrites?"

I could do this. "All of it," I said. "If you have time."

He nodded, picking up the script I'd left on the table. "When does filming start?"

I plunked the beers down, grabbed my slice. "Three weeks, though we start rehearsals next Tuesday."

"And it'll be shot over at the studio?"

"Most of it," I said around a bite. "We'll also have a few weeks in New Mexico."

We took a few minutes to talk locations and length, comparing notes about where we'd both been. By the time we'd both finished our pizzas, we were onto our second beers. He took a long sip of his. "I did a shoot once at White Sands. My model freaked out because she got sand on her skin."

I lift a brow. "Seriously?"

His lips curved. "She didn't like it when I pointed out that it wasn't actually sand, but gypsum."

"Smartass," I muttered.

"Not disagreeing with you," he said.

"But also, I appreciate your conviction to being scientifically correct."

Damon laughed. "I'm glad you appreciate my dedication to learning."

I snorted.

He chuckled.

We stared at each other for a long moment and I felt the past pressing on me again, sitting heavy on my lungs, tapdancing on the back of my tongue. I had to clear the air. I couldn't—

"Don't," he whispered.

I stopped, stared up at him agape.

He shook his head. "I'm sorry, I didn't mean it like that. I just—don't feel like you owe me anything. Last night was . . . fucking fantastic, if I'm being honest, but being your friend is also fantastic and if that's all we can be, then I'm fine, Ed. I don't need more than you're able to give."

Soft. Sweet. Kind.

Damon.

I traced shapes in the condensation on the outside of the beer bottle. "I can't be more than friends with you," I whispered. "Last night *was* fantastic, but . . . I think you saw enough to realize that I can't be in a relationship." A beat as I met his eyes. "I won't let myself go there."

Damon studied me for several moments. "Won't let yourself go there?" he asked. "Or let yourself go there *again?*"

My fingers froze mid-circle, and I forced my eyes to stay on his. "Again."

Silence, then the beer bottle hit the table and his fisted hands moved to his hips. "I want to ask who I should kill," he began.

I rested my hand on his knee. "Then you'd have to dig him up and kill him again."

His gaze was furious, but at my words, his hands flattened out and he dropped his chin to his chest, which expanded and fell on a long exhale.

"I'm okay, Damon," I murmured.

Chocolate eyes sparking fire, but he didn't say what he had every right to. Which was that, clearly, I *wasn't* okay because of the way I'd acted earlier that day. Instead, he just stared at me, fury in his expression, body stiff and unmoving.

Except for his chest.

That kept lifting and falling in rapid succession, his staccato breaths the only noise in the room.

Then his hand dropped onto mine, loosely gripping my fingers where they still rested on his knee. "I'm sorry you went through whatever it was that was bad enough to mark you so thoroughly. I'm sorry that I pushed this morning. I'm—"

I squeezed his leg lightly. "Me, too," I said. "But I promised myself a long time ago I would stop apologizing for what he did."

"I—"

"And if it's cool with you, I'd like to put the past where it belongs and focus on the good things I have going on in my life," I said. "The first of which is having a friend like you who cares." I waited until he glanced up at me and smiled. "The second being"—I slipped my hand free and tapped the script on the table—"having the ability to actually complain about rewrites because I'm working in my dream job and doing films rather than cat food commercials."

Damon's jaw clenched despite my levity though he nodded, albeit tightly. "I'm glad you have that, too."

"I'm also lucky to have someone read those rewritten lines with me." I picked up the script, handed it to him. "Hint, hint."

His lips curved just the slightest bit, and he reached over and took it from me. "Okay, sweetheart." His smile expanded. "Or should I say okay, demander?"

"I prefer the first," I teased. "But I stand by the second."

He grinned. I giggled.

And then we both set down our beers and got to work running the lines.

Damon was patient, feeding them to me when I faltered with the new material, but not just giving them all to me freely.

He made me work; testing my memory and helping them stick in my brain.

That wasn't even mentioning the vast amount of accents he could do. He colored more emotions into the script than I'd been able to do in my mind, and that was saying something. I really liked the story and had brought it to life in my brain, complete with mental images and voices.

"How are you so good at this?" I accused about halfway through. "I'm starting to think you moved to L.A. so you could pursue acting yourself."

He laughed. "Not at all," he said, turning the page and pausing. "My sister was the theater geek, that's it. End of story." His eyes darted away from mine. And was that a blush? "Okay, now Madeline says—"

I pinned him with a stare. "Why am I not thinking that's the end of the story, based on your avoidance?"

"She says, 'And I don't know why—'"

"Damon."

"'You're looking at me that way.' And Todd replies—"

"*Damon.*"

He froze, shoulders rising, eyes still on the script, but . . . yes, that definitely was a hint of blush on his cheeks?

Oh my God.

I yanked the script out of his hands.

"Spill it, buster."

He snagged it back. "'You can't expect me to—'"

"Damon Alexander Garcia, don't you dare try and hold out on me."

"I'm not holding—"

I narrowed my eyes. "Yes, you are."

"I'm—"

"Remember that time I told you you'd drank too much

tequila and were going to have a massive hangover the next day?"

A grunt.

"Or when you'd eaten that chocolate cake too fast?"

If there was such a thing as flipping a script page aggressively, then Damon did it. "As I was saying—"

"Or when you were taking on too much and needed a vacation?"

"Pot meet kettle," he muttered.

"Hence, the reason we took that long weekend to Miami, remember?"

He reached for his beer, guzzled down a mouthful, eyes carefully avoiding mine. "Yeah, so what?"

"So, I *know* you, Damon. I know when you've eaten too much, or drank too much, or worked too much."

"That may be true but—"

"I also know when you're lying about something," I went on. "You know I do. It's the same reason I knew you were near burnout and going to be sick to your stomach. It's why I know that hint of blush on your cheeks means that you're holding out on me."

He sighed, dropped the script to his lap. "Eden."

I sighed, dropped my hands to my lap. "Damon."

We faced off for several long moments.

But I wasn't caving. He wasn't telling me everything. I knew that, without a doubt, and based on his reluctance to dish, I also knew that what he was holding back was going to be good.

Really good.

He sighed again and flopped back against the cushions. "First, I don't know how you know or why I let you convince me to tell you these things."

I grinned and clapped my hands together. "OMG. Is this going to be as good as your sisters shaving your eyebrows right before you went on a date with the girl you'd been crushing on for months?"

"First," he muttered. "*That* was abuse. Second—" He snorted. "It *was* pretty funny."

I giggled. "Yes, and well-deserved if I'm remembering what you told me you did correctly."

"You mean me swapping their shampoo with hair bleach?"

I nodded fervently. "That was probably the most devious of all the sibling torture I've heard you guys committed."

"I was only trying to one-up them after they'd superglued my butt to the toilet seat."

"I—" I broke off on a chuckle and shook my head. "You lot were relentless."

"My poor mother," he said in agreement. "Though, did I ever tell you about the time she made cookies and *accidentally* swapped the sugar for salt?"

I shook my head.

"We had this rule in my house. My mom cooked and we ate it without complaint," he said. "We weren't poor, by any means. But it wasn't like we could afford to throw out meals just because we didn't want to eat our broccoli, you know?"

I nodded, loving how his face gentled when he spoke of his family.

"So anyway, we all choked down those salt cookies, not saying a damn word because the ingredients were pricey and my mom worked a lot, so her being able to bake at all meant that she'd taken the time."

"Insane practical joking aside," I said. "It sounds like you were good kids."

"Yeah, we were," he said. "For the most part."

He grinned and I smiled back. "Me, too."

"I can't imagine you ever doing anything bad," he said, tugging on a lock of my hair. "You're too nice."

I *hadn't* done anything bad. Not ever. I'd been a rule follower from day one. But being a rule follower had also gotten me into the situation I'd nearly died trying to survive. So now I was less about abiding by the rules and more about being a nice person, but not allowing myself to be used or hurt.

Armor.

Yup.

Closed down.

Most certainly.

But an asshole?

No. I wasn't that.

Damon tucked a strand behind my ear, seeming to realize my thoughts had drifted somewhere else, somewhere unpleasant. "So, anyway, back to the cookies. I mean, we must have choked down six or seven each, my dad included. Not one of us made a peep of protest or complaint, but I swear, we pounded a gallon of milk faster than those cookies."

"And you never said anything?" I asked.

He shook his head. "No, none of us wanted to hurt her feelings."

"That's sweet."

"It's devious," he said, "and I'll tell you why. My mom knew we wouldn't say anything. She. Knew. Which is why she swapped the sugar and salt on purpose."

I gasped. "No."

"Yup."

"Apparently my dad had scared her that morning before work, jumping out from behind her car and making her spill her coffee. She hadn't had time for a replacement because she'd spent an hour before work unsticking my ass from the toilet seat because of my sisters—"

"And circling back to you and your devious use of bleach."

A flash of white. "I think my mom was the devious one, and her deviousness existed in the form of salt."

I laughed. "Were they really that bad?"

He shuddered. "They were horrible." Snagging his beer, he lifted it to his lips and drank deeply. "I swear, just thinking about that story and I can taste them all over again." He mimed scraping off his tongue. "It's an awful cross to bear."

My laughter bubbled up in me, filling my lungs, escaping my lips, and Damon joined in, both of us giggling like loons for several minutes before we managed to get under control.

I wiped a finger under each eye. "I think I'm glad I didn't have siblings," I said. "Being an only child is the way to go."

He shook his head. "They weren't so bad."

"Superglue? Eyebrows?"

"Okay," he admitted. "They were bad." A beat. "But so was I."

"True."

"And plus, the salt cookies taught us a lesson."

I lifted a brow. "Yeah? What could that possibly be?"

"To only pull pranks that wouldn't bother my mom."

I snorted. "So, the cookies didn't reform you so much as teach you to be smarter?"

He considered that then nodded. "Yes, I guess that's exactly right. We didn't stop with the pranks, only did them where she —and her coffee—wouldn't be affected."

"Smart."

"Learned survivalists more like."

I tugged the script from his hands. "So, is that where you learned to do all the voices? From pranking your sisters?"

Damon plunked his bottle on the table. "I gave you salt cookies, and you're still demanding more?"

"Salt cookies isn't voice actor training," I pointed out.

He wrinkled his nose.

"Come on, Damon," I coaxed. "I have a box of cookies in the pantry and they have the proper amount of salt-to-sugar ratio."

A put-upon sigh.

"Okay, fine. I was in a few plays."

I waited for more of an explanation and when none came, I lifted a brow.

"Okay, okay," he muttered. "Those plays were more like family productions. As in, every Christmas, my parents picked a play that we'd put on for the family. There were lots of different ones—*A Christmas Carol, Annie,* and the like. I'm the youngest, and so I played the younger roles."

Nodding, I said, "That makes sense."

"Well, I was really into it and the year I played Annie, I insisted on having my hair permed, not wearing a wig."

"Okaay . . ."

He sighed. "Do I really have to—?"

"Yes."

"I thought it was cool growing up. It was fun to hang with my sisters and do something productive. We even did it through middle school."

"Why am I sensing a *but* here?"

"Probably because my sisters decided to screen our production of *Annie* for my entire middle school, complete with me in a dress and perm and singing my little heart out about tomorrow."

"I'm not getting why that was bad?"

His expression was dark. "Because it was middle school and kids are assholes in any school, but they're most especially assholes in *middle* school."

"You were teased?"

He shrugged. "Of course, I was. But the worst part was whoever printed out a still from that video and pasted my permed-up-hairband-wearing head all over school."

"That does sound pretty awful."

"It was worse than the eyebrows."

I pressed my lips flat to smother my smile.

He saw anyway. "I see how it is. You laugh at my pain?"

I shook my head. "No, of course not." But my chest was rattling with suppressed laughter.

"See if I bring you pizza again," he muttered.

I stopped. "No, I'm n-not l-laughing," I stammered. "It w-was a horrible thing t-to do—"

"Eden."

"Uh-huh?"

He held up the script. "Let's get back to work."

I didn't think at that point. I just let the laughter rip and threw my arms around his shoulders, hugging him tight. "I'm not laughing *at* you," I said.

"Uh-huh, sure," he replied, but his body was shaking with mirth, too. "See if next time I put my acting skills at your disposal."

"No," I demanded, pulling back. "Don't do that. You're too good—"

"Nope, flattery will do you no good right about now."

I pouted. "I'll be good. I promise."

He shook his head. "Just be you, Ed. That's all I want."

His words curled around my heart, stroking gently, hugging lightly. Such a wonderful man.

So much not for me.

"Fine," I said, deliberately ignoring that last thought. We were moving on. That was the only way. Done. End of story. No more angst about the decision. "Then I at least promise not to pay someone to Photoshop a curly wig on your head and paste it in front of an *Annie* poster then put it on my Instagram."

"Why pay someone when I could do that for free?" he deadpanned.

We stared at each other. His lips hitched up. Mine curved in response.

Then we were both laughing.

And it was like the old Eden and Damon again.

I was glad.

Really, I was.

SEVEN

Damon

I ABIDED by my promise to leave Eden's house early and then followed through on my promise to lie in bed for the next twenty-four hours and catch up on bad TV and sleep.

Turned out I wasn't so good at tolerating the bad television part, but I did a damned good job at sleeping.

Hadn't had much of that over the last months.

I'd been booked solid, traveling the world and shooting everyone from the latest Oscar winner's pregnancy shoot—and Artie Miller had been absolutely radiant, so beautiful, in fact, that she'd agreed to sell the image as a cover for a fancy fashion magazine—to images for men's health publications.

Speaking of that fancy magazine Artie had just graced the cover of, I'd been busy working for them, too. I'd begun six months back at their studios in New York then moved on to Aruba—which I'd paired with another couple of shoots, one for a sports spread in an athlete-driven magazine and another for a series of photographs of a certain reality TV star who was going to use them for a new line of swimsuits and loungewear. After that, I'd been in London, Copenhagen, Iceland, and Australia, until I'd finally come to L.A. to photograph Artie, just over a month before.

She'd been reticent at first, thinking that pregnancy shoots were showy and self-indulgent, but her husband, Pierce, had coaxed her into celebrating the moment. I was glad he'd stepped in.

There was something special about a woman with child—that radiant glow, the life growing within her somehow making her bloom into something even more multifaceted. It was beautiful and Artie even more so, especially because she was so confident in her body. She had been game for everything.

Naked? Sure.

Draped in flowers. Why not?

A strategically placed strip of diaphanous material? Great. Done.

It had been easy and fun and filled with laughter, one of the best shoots I'd done all year and the perfect way to wrap up my long-ass run.

Now I'd cleared my schedule for a couple of months, would enjoy the break, explore southern and central California, and then take some time to visit my family up near the Oregon border.

There were sure to be some interesting characters in the town more famous for pot and naked communes. I'd be able to get some unique portraits in.

So there, I'd been in L.A. for less than a week, I had no work demands on my schedule, and I had a plan moving forward. Good. Done.

Maybe I'd start with Joshua Tree. I'd grown up in California, home being a small town just east of San Francisco, but I'd never been to the national park in the desert, never seen the strange-looking Yucca trees. It'd be good to tick off some of those quintessential California things—or quintessential because I'd grown up here and I wasn't counting the touristy spots of Disneyland, Yosemite, the Golden Gate, and the like.

I wanted to drive up Highway 1. I wanted to stop in Solvang and get some butter cookies, compare them with their truly Danish counterparts I'd eaten in Copenhagen. I wanted to hike through Lassen. I wanted to take some time and just wander.

But also . . . Eden.

I wanted to be close to Eden.

Except, she had a life and she was going to be busy with her own career and . . . she wanted to be just friends.

I could be friends from a distance. We'd managed that for years.

Maybe I wanted more, maybe I'd seen my chance and leaped . . . and that hadn't worked out. So, now I should step back. I should focus on friendship and my plan-that-wasn't-a-plan to bum around California for six months.

I should go back to weekly phone calls and leave Eden to keep wearing her armor.

It wasn't for show.

It was functional.

She needed it. I got that. Really, I did. I understood that with every brain cell in my sometimes-malfunctioning male brain.

I grinned at her teasing words from the night before.

Eden was funny. Fuck, she could make me laugh like no other. She was smart and gorgeous and strong and . . .

I didn't want to leave L.A.

Or rather, I didn't want to leave an L.A. with Eden in it.

I wanted to be here. To be with *her*.

Except . . . she didn't want to be with me.

Not in the way I wanted. I needed to accept that. I needed to be what was good for her and—

I jumped out of bed and stalked to the bathroom.

Fuck that shit.

What? Was I going to be a coward and just step aside and not even try? Was I going to throw away the connection, the friendship, the feelings that had grown so deep? No. I *couldn't* do that.

I was here. She was here.

We'd taken a step.

It had backfired, yes, but no relationship was smooth sailing. If I was smart and patient and could just play my cards right, then maybe I could have a chance at something more than just friendship. Bottom line, she had to feel something for me or she wouldn't have been so emotionally invested, wouldn't have texted to make things right or had me over at her house last night. Our friendship, our *relationship* was important to her.

That was something.

That wasn't me being a one-night fuck who she'd thrust out the front door the next morning.

I meant more to her than that.

I needed to remember that, to hold it close and keep my mind clear. I needed to be smart and patient and . . .

I needed to not give up.

Well, I was just a small-town kid from a middle-class family. I wasn't special or unique or exceptionally talented. Oh, I wasn't falsely modest. I was realistic. I did my job and did it well. No drama. No ego. No taking the easy way out.

That was how I'd made my way from small town to big city, from county fair exhibitions to big-time Hollywood contracts.

I put my head down and got shit done.

So yeah, not giving up was kind of my life's motto.

EIGHT

Eden

"SHE'S BEAUTIFUL," I whispered, smiling at Artie while cradling their newborn baby against my chest. I ran a finger across her cheek, feeling the silky skin and my insides twinging with an old pain.

An old pain that would never be soothed.

Because I was . . . empty.

Except, maybe, I didn't have to be.

Wrong. It wasn't empty. It was safer.

But why did safer not feel better? It used to be so comfortable and easy and empowering, in a way. Now, it felt constricting, weak . . . especially with the snoozing newborn in my arms, so vulnerable, the people who loved her the most trusting me with the precious bundle.

Little Daphne—because Artie was actually Artemis and she and Pierce had decided to stick with the Greek names—stirred in my arms, a soft mewl emerging from pink rosebud lips.

"Yes, she is beautiful," Pierce said, scooping her out of my arms and doing some cradling of his own. "Just like her mama."

Artie smiled, leaning over to tuck the blanket around little Daphne, not because it seemed at threat of unraveling, but because she couldn't help herself from touching and caring for and protecting her baby . . . even if that was from a tiny perceived dip in temperature.

Unlike my parents.

Be quiet. Don't run, for fuck's sake! Don't make a fuss or question. Be respectful.

Be a lady.

Well, I *hadn't* made a fuss, had I?

I hadn't stopped Tim from doing what he wanted. I hadn't run. I hadn't been loud. I'd let him respectfully take what he wanted.

And perhaps it wasn't precisely ladylike, but I'd also been starving for attention since I hadn't received any from my parents. Tim had been there. He'd given me that attention, made me feel special, and for my selfishness, my needing that attention, I'd paid a very heavy price.

The memories were oppressive, sitting on my lungs, making my throat burn. I popped to my feet. I wasn't going to have a meltdown in front of the people who'd done so much for me. *Breathe.* I sucked in some air, steadied myself. "I should go," I said, "let you both get some rest."

"You don't have to—"

"I have some lines to go over," I said, and it wasn't *exactly* a lie. All I knew was that I had to get out of there before I did something, before I ruined—

Enough.

Forcing a smile, I hugged Artie, kissed Pierce on the cheek, and brushed my fingers across Daphne's cheek.

"Eden."

"I hope you get some sleep."

Artie snorted. "With this little one? Not likely."

A complaint, but one filled with teasing love.

I picked up my purse, heart aching, but forced lightness in my tone. "Meh. I've seen how little sleep you guys run on. You'll both be fine."

Pierce cupped Artie's cheek and smiled down at his wife. The love in that glance took my breath away, seized my lungs, absolutely made my heart hurt.

I wanted *that*.

The yearning was a lightning rod.

I wanted someone to look at me like Pierce did to Artie, love shining in his eyes, affection written across his face, expression so soft and—

I *could* have that.

With Damon.

But no, I *couldn't*. I couldn't risk going down that road. Damon was a good person, and wanting something between us would only end in heartbreak.

Yet I still wanted it.

I was desperate for something that would only destroy me.

Artie glanced over at me, concern overtaking her expression, and I knew my face must have shown my longing, my fear, my desire, all mingled together. "Eden?"

Thankfully, I was close to the front door. "See you guys soon!" I called and high-tailed it out of there.

But not fast enough.

Artie knocked on my driver's side window before I could pull out of the driveway, and I felt a pang of guilt for making a woman who'd recently given birth chase after me.

Still sighed before I rolled down the window though.

She stared at my face for a long moment. "Don't do this to yourself, honey," she murmured.

"I'm fine," I said. "I promise."

I *was* fine. I was *always* fine. I always found a way to get through.

"I know you're fine," she said, hand resting on top of mine on the steering wheel for a brief moment. "I was fine, too." A squeeze. "But consider that you could be great, Eden. That you *deserve* to be great."

She stepped back and waved as I opened my mouth to protest, to agree, to spill my guts, who knew?

Either way, I didn't get a chance to express any of that.

Artie waved one more time then disappeared into the house.

And I sat in her driveway for long moments before gathering myself and driving away.

But I couldn't deny that something inside of me had shifted.

A WEEK since I'd seen baby Daphne and I was feeling . . . unsettled.

I was dreaming of Tim, of that time when I'd been so young and vulnerable, excited and hopeful for a happy ending, to find someone who would love me and—

It wasn't to be.

I relied on myself, lived my life by myself.

That was better.

Except . . . I wasn't really by myself, was I?

I had Artie and Pierce. I had Damon. I had my agent, my publicist, Maggie. I had loads of people . . . all of whom I paid or who'd been responsible for my paycheck.

With the exception of Damon.

No connection aside from . . . a connection.

We'd done Pizza Night the previous evening and it had been light, almost impersonal. He'd shown me some pictures he'd taken at Joshua Tree National Park and for as much as he liked to tell me that he wasn't a good nature photographer, his shots of the harsh landscape and alien-esque trees were stark but beautiful.

But he hadn't stayed long, just for carbs, photos, and one episode of a documentary called *McMillion$*—it followed the McDonald's Monopoly scandal and was as crazy as it was interesting. But Damon and I were still tentative after our night together, after the scene in my bedroom.

He hadn't worn long sleeves, and the Band-Aids on his arm were a blatant reminder of what had happened between us.

It made me quiet.

And sad.

And . . . the persistent ping in the back of my mind telling me that I was missing out, that I could have more if I only just—

Enough.

I pulled out the script and my pencil and started going through it again. There was a scene toward the climax that was going to be tricky to balance the comedy aspect of the film with my character's growth.

And yes, I understood it was a comedy, but without proper growth and development of the main characters, it was going to be boring and very one-note for the audience.

My phone rang just as I'd turned to the scene, and speaking of people I paid, Maggie, my publicist, was on the phone.

"Hey," I said, putting her on speaker.

Maggie was an awesome publicist, had first worked with athletes, training up in San Francisco with a big firm called Prestige Media Group, but had then transitioned to celebrities and Hollywood and was now running her own company.

Artie had recommended her to me, and it had been one of the best things I'd done for my career.

Maggie made it so I didn't have to think about anything except for acting.

No games. No going out to be *seen*. I could just be me, sitting at home in my PJs, picking the films I wanted, and not overexposed by unnecessary press and interviews.

So, yeah, maybe I gave Maggie a paycheck, but I was also lucky enough to have her steady presence in my life.

"You ready to go?" she asked. "I'm not interrupting?"

"I'm good," I said, setting the script aside. I was fussing and tinkering when I just needed to stop. Rehearsals would begin tomorrow, and I needed to be fresh enough that my performance wouldn't be stale.

"Good. Just a couple of things. The studio wants to get a couple of publicity shots, so they were hoping you could do that Monday or Tuesday." A pause, and we'd been working together long enough that I knew Maggie was waiting for me to chime in if I had a problem with that. Since I didn't and I remained silent, she went on, "*People* wanted to see if you'd give a quote for the importance of female representation in Hollywood. I agreed, since Artie is doing it as well. It'll be a bit of a fluff piece, but it fits in with your brand. I'll put something together and you can approve." Another beat. Another moment of me keeping quiet since that was fine.

Maggie kept working down her list, all minor commitments, all easy to do now since I was in L.A. for the time being.

"You're easy today," she said.

"I'm easy *every* day."

She laughed. "That's true enough. You never create drama for me."

"That's because I don't have a personal life."

"You do give me a challenge in that way."

I frowned. "What?"

"It's all about image, babe, you know that," Maggie said. "And you're the Queen of Single."

My brows drew further together. "Um—"

"Oh, no," Maggie said. "I'm not trying to say that's a bad thing at all. You do you. Be happy. Be single. It's just that the press sometimes loves nothing better than a good relationship story, and so I spend half of my time killing stories about your potential boyfriends or fiancés, rather than talking about all of the good things you're doing, work wise."

"Oh."

"And the shitty thing is that if you *were* in a relationship, it wouldn't be any different. Every other story would be about when you two were getting married or is Eden Larsen wearing a ring or is that a baby bump?"

Slice.

Slice.

Slice.

Married. Ring. Baby.

Damn, the past would just not stay tucked away.

I heard Maggie suck in a breath and realized that I'd been silent too long. "I . . . uh . . . that would be fine if you *were* pregnant or secretly engaged . . ."

The careful question at the end of her trailing off snapped me out of it. "Sorry," I said. "You won't be able to use your Secret Agent Ninja PR skills on me right now. I'm not engaged or pregnant. I'm not even dating anyone right now, let alone having a sex life."

One night didn't count as a sex life, right?

"It would be okay if you were."

I snorted.

"Sorry, that sounded asshole-y," Maggie said, contrite now. "I just meant—"

"I know," I said. "I'm just doing my part to not be easy *all* of the time. Okay, so let me play celebrity gossip columnist. What about you? How's Ben?"

A sigh. "Ben is now firmly in the category of ex."

"Ugh. I'm sorry." Her tone told me it hadn't been a pleasant breakup.

"He decided that being tied to one woman was too much pressure for him . . . and also that he wanted to sell my lingerie on eBay."

"Ew."

"*Dirty* lingerie."

"Double ew."

"I know." A beat. "Men suck."

"Yes," I agreed, but even as I commiserated with her on the suckage of men, I couldn't help but think that not *all* of them were bad.

Pierce staring at Artie, love all over his face.

Damon smiling down at me from my porch, pizza boxes in hand.

Tim's angry eyes, fist descending—

I blinked, caught the tail end of Maggie's sentence

". . . and so then I threw all of *his* underwear out of the window," Maggie said. "God, I've seen them do that in movies, but actually doing it in real life was *so* satisfying."

The image of cool and collected Maggie launching underwear out her window made me laugh, made the past fade back away.

"Please tell me they were tighty-whities."

"Unfortunately, Ben was strictly a boxer brief man."

"Disappointing."

"In so, so many ways." Then she sighed and shifted back to business, promising to touch base with me about the shoot on Monday or Tuesday, wishing me luck for rehearsals, telling me I was going to kill it.

Supportive. Sharing. Funny. Caring.

All the things a friend would do.

By the time I thanked her and hung up, I realized that maybe I wasn't quite as alone as I'd thought.

A Month Later

Rehearsals were completed, filming had started, and I'd quickly gone from being beyond excited to begin shooting to absolutely dreading showing up to work every day.

My male costar was . . .

An ass.

Grant Seagurio had been the hottest thing in town about five years before, lead billing on every movie he'd made, films hitting the top of the box office, paparazzi trailing his every move.

And now . . . a little of that star power had dimmed.

He'd headed a few busts, but that wasn't what he was struggling to overcome. Nope, what had really shuttered his fandom was the video of him yelling at a valet. Okay, not so much as just yelling, but screaming, throwing things, kicking over a trash can, and then running over the foot of the poor valet.

All for grinding the gears of his Ferrari.

Oh, man. He had it so tough.

I snorted to myself as I watched him on set. I'd been reticent to work with him after the incident, but it had been several years without anything else happening to make headlines and so I'd hoped he'd grown up, grown out of the asshole-ness, especially when jobs had begun to dry up. Clearly, I'd been wrong. Nothing seemed to faze him. Grant's ego was something to behold, and I felt like I'd been around Hollywood and the model world long enough to have seen some huge ass egos.

Grant's was . . . on a whole other level.

He yelled at the makeup artist for having made him look too shiny in one shot, never mind that he'd batted the girl away when she'd come in to touch up. He screamed at the boom operator for having had the nerve to shift positions and distract him. He'd argued with the director about the shot list and been late to set when he'd disagreed.

And he'd . . . barely spoken a word to me, even though we were supposed to somehow be creating chemistry on screen.

I'd heard him rage into his cell that first day after rehearsals about how his agent had forced him to work with a former model.

As though it were the lowest thing that could possibly happen to him.

Meanwhile, it was going to be *my* name as top billing because *my* agent was good and because . . . well, I'd become the bigger star over the last year.

Normally, I didn't give a damn about things like that.

But with Grant being the way he was, wreaking havoc and ejaculating his ego all over the set—

I bit back a chuckle.

Ejaculating his ego?

I'd been watching too many Netflix comedy specials of late, apparently. Though it didn't seem like much of it had rubbed off on me if I was passing the time by making internal jokes about ejaculating egos.

Or maybe, *too* much of it was rubbing off on me.

First stop, rom-com. Next, comedy tour.

Yeah, right. Stifling a snort, I continued watching the scene unfold in front of me. So ejaculating egos might not be the best metaphor, but I got a few extra points for alliteration.

Hey. No judgment, okay?

Sometimes there was a lot of downtime on set, and since I couldn't rip the microphone out of the boom operator's hands, cross over to Grant, and then use the long metal rod to beat Grant senseless, I had to satisfy myself with imagining the pleasure.

And ejaculating, rods, and pleasure.

Heh.

But speaking of ejaculating, rods, and pleasure, I was horny. Like *really* horny. In fact, if I were being honest about the amount of my horniness, I was more pent-up than I could ever remember.

Or maybe a more apt description was that I was more pent-up than my early twenties addiction to all things Chris Hemsworth.

Okay, not gonna lie, I still had that addiction.

I was just slightly *more* addicted to a certain chocolate-eyed photographer, whose quiet and velvet-lined voice never failed to make me shiver and who'd been perfectly friendly while somehow making me want him even more.

And speaking of ejaculating, Damon's cock had been—

"Absolutely *not!*" Grant exploded. "I will *not* do it again. That was perfect, and I will not let some two-bit director tell me how to do my job . . ."

My cell was in the pocket of my chair, and I felt it buzz.

Thank God.

Not only that I'd remembered to put it on silent, because imagine the conniption that Grant would have had if it wasn't, but also that because I hadn't left it in my dressing room and now I had something to distract me from the disaster that was unfolding in front of me.

My phone vibrated again, and I saw that Damon had texted.

Then immediately felt my lips curve up into a smile.

Things had gone back to the way they were before, well, almost exactly like they were before. Damon had returned to being my friend, randomly texting me throughout the week, though our standing Thursday night phone call had morphed into Pizza Night at my house.

We'd tried one time at his condo, but he lived . . . slightly Spartanly, should I say. Or to be more specific, I wasn't impressed by his lumpy couch and bare pantry. Though, he'd at least bought the good beer and had promised that he'd have me over when the stuff he'd shipped over from the U.K. had arrived.

But it was either his place or mine, because going out to eat wasn't exactly feasible for me at the moment. Or at least, not feasible without pictures documenting the event ending up splashed across the gossip sites. I didn't want to get all dressed up, to do my hair and makeup. I wanted to be in my pajamas or sweatpants and an oversized sweater with my air conditioning blasting—and not as a protection from Damon, or protecting me from *my* reaction to Damon, but because they were cozy.

And because we were friends. Just friends.

No lingering touches. No more sex on the kitchen table.

No awkward silences or limited explanations of the past.

It was just him and me. Just as we should have been.

So, why did it feel like I was missing out on something?

Buzz. Buzz.

I blinked, pulled myself out of my head, and focused on Damon's messages on my cell.

How's the Ego?

(I know you're on set for the day, so just call or text when you can)

I was smiling already because Damon was texting, but his use of our nickname for Grant had me stifling giggles. Because, man, was it apropos. But then my cell vibrated once more.

Also, can we reschedule Pizza Night tomorrow? I have a date.

My smile faded.

A date?

Damon had a date?

What the fuck? How dare he have the nerve to go on a—

"No, Eden," I muttered, so maybe I was growing used to having him in my life frequently, but it wasn't like I was ready to forget everything that happened to me and get myself a boyfriend.

Even if that boyfriend was Damon? my brain asked

Yes. Even then.

"This is a good thing," I murmured. "He's moving on. Just as it should be." I sucked in a breath, forced my fingers to type out a reply.

Sure, we can reschedule. Want to do Friday night instead?

A few moments before another buzz.

I can't. I'm leaving Friday for my trip.

We'd just talked the day before, and he'd told me he was going to take a trip up the coast, leave on Saturday, make a long weekend of it. Had that changed already?

I thought you were going on Saturday?

Also, why did my heart pulse at the thought of him making plans without me?

Changed my mind. So next week then?

Because I was slowly going insane, wanting things I had no business wanting. Sighing, I shoved down the urge to revolt and forced myself to remember this was a good thing. He was moving on, just like I'd asked. We were friends—

Except, date?

Fucking really?

I wrinkled my nose and then I tucked all the extraneous emotions away and sent him back a response.

Next week is great.

Then I turned off my cell, shoved it back into the pocket of the chair, and returned my focus to Grant and bearing witness to the insanity of his ego trip.

It was going to be a really long day.

I HADN'T HEARD from Damon.

Okay, fine. That wasn't entirely fair.

He'd texted me a couple of images, pretty shots of the coast and one striking photo of a child climbing a tree, but that was it. He hadn't given me any words or responded to me asking about his date, and he hadn't texted me to ask me what I wanted on our pizza for our weekly hangout tonight.

He *always* texted to ask.

Even though my response was always the same.

Extra pepperoni and don't skimp on the garlic bread.

He never did.

But now . . . radio silence.

"Shit," I muttered, grabbing my cell and pulling up Door-Dash. I'd order my own damn pizza *and* garlic bread, and I'd watch a bad movie all on my own.

I didn't need yummy-smelling, velvet-voice Damon Garcia.

No ma'am.

No—

The doorbell rang.

Since I was in the middle of a huff, I didn't stop to glance through the window to check who it was, and actually, I was feeling a little off. Not just emotional, but also really tired and cranky.

Though that probably just circled me right back to emotional.

Plus, my boobs hurt.

And also another thing to be cranky about. My period was afoot.

Ah, to be a woman.

Such a joy.

Anyway, I'd already turned the knob and was pulling the door open by the time I'd realized that was a stupid thing to do. "Shit," I muttered and slammed it shut.

Then I looked out the window.

Then I saw Damon, balancing some pizza boxes.

At which point, I realized he'd seen me acting like an idiot.

Cool.

"Shit," I muttered, reaching for the knob, just as the bell rang again. I pulled it open and stood back.

"I thought you were holding last week against me," he murmured, lips curving up at the edges. "I didn't want to cancel. I just . . ."

"It's fine, it's fine," I hurried to say. "And I'm sorry I

slammed the door on you. I was distracted and didn't look through the window."

"You should be apologizing to the pizza," he said, holding up the boxes. "Your extra garlic bread almost hit the dirt"—he glanced down at the porch as he stepped inside—"or the concrete, rather."

"Meh." I locked up behind him, already feeling better because he was nearby. And no, I wasn't contemplating that feeling further. I was going to be blissfully ignorant and just pretend my heart hadn't expanded with joy when I'd seen him there standing outside my door. *Good plan, Eden. Can't backfire at all.* "Shut up," I said under my breath to my ever-spinning mind and then pushed everything extraneous from my thoughts and focused on Damon. And the garlic bread. "That's what the five-second rule is for."

"You okay?"

I nodded. "Just tired."

"Hmm." He stared at me for a heartbeat then did some nodding of his own before heading into the kitchen. "You do know that the five-second rule is not a thing, right?"

I grinned. "Yes, I *do* know that," I said, moving past him as we undertook our usual routine of gathering plates and napkins, pulling beers from the fridge. "I know it because you made me watch that stupid *Mythbusters* episode three times."

Damon dished up slices then carried the boxes and plates into the family room. "It sounds like you'll need to watch it another time if you think it's so stupid."

I shuddered, grabbed the beers and napkins. "God, no. It wasn't stupid. I just objected to the volume of viewing."

"Volume of viewing?" he asked. "You one of those fancy actors who warm up with those alliteration word games, are you now?"

I sat down on the couch with a sigh. God, I was tired. But it had been a long and trying week with Grant. Though, thankfully, the dailies looked good. Apparently, hate behind the scenes could translate well enough to mimic desire.

A desire to throttle one's co-star, that was.

"Don't get me started," I said. "I've been spending my week trying to come up with a better alliteration than ego ejaculating."

He froze, slice an inch from his mouth. "Um, what?"

I shook my head, took a bite of my own. God, that was good. After I'd chewed, I explained. "He's like a cat pissing everywhere, marking everyone with his ego, but that's not an e-word and so . . ."

"Ego ejaculating."

A shrug. "Unfortunately, yes."

Damon studied me for a long moment. "That's not all of it."

My cheeks went hot. I could feel them burning and knew they'd be bright red. Thanks, karma for making me a redhead. That blush would be flared crimson across my cheeks, staining my chest. Not cute.

Also, making it very obvious when I was lying.

Which Damon knew. So he just lifted an eyebrow, stared, and waited.

"Dammit," I said on an exasperated huff. "Fine. It started with ejaculating ego and then I added to it."

"Added what exactly?"

"Eagerly ejaculating ego elucidates earnestly excessive aches." I stopped then shrugged when I saw his expression had frozen into one of shock. I was in it already, might as well tell him all of it. "I couldn't think of an e-word for ache, but give me time."

He was still silent, still frozen, but then his eyes warmed, his lips curled up into a smile and—

He burst into laughter. It was raucous and loud, and it

wasn't his soft voice or his sharp ordering tone or even his teasing intonation that never failed to make me feel lighter inside. This was . . .

I'd delighted him.

And I liked that, too, *too* much.

But before I could dwell on that for too long, he'd gotten himself under control. "I'll work on finding a suitable e-word for ache."

I smiled despite myself. "Shut up and eat your pizza."

He obliged, taking another bite before talking around the food. "I *am* eating." He shoved my plate at me. "Now, you."

"You're disgusting," I said, batting his hand away. "Chew with your mouth closed."

"Meh," he said. "We don't stand on ceremony. Not between us friends."

Was it just me? Or had he emphasized the word *friends*? I paused, setting the plate back down, ignoring the way that made me feel. It was this movie. I was just tired from dealing with the Ego and—

"Are you all right?"

I nodded. "Fine. Just tired."

See? If I said it aloud, it had to be true.

"Well, let's fuel that very talented actor's body"—he opened the lid on the box—"with garlic bread."

My stomach did a funny dip when the smell of garlic hit my nose.

Then I was on my feet, my hand clamped over my mouth.

"Eden?" Damon jumped up, too, reaching for me. "What's the matter—?"

I brushed him off and ran for the closest bathroom. My knees hit the rug by the toilet, and I . . .

Well, thankfully, I hadn't eaten much, because it all came up and landed in that white porcelain bowl. Awful. It tasted awful, felt horrible, and the usual relief that came from the after-effects of puking didn't come.

My stomach still churned.

A hand rested lightly on my back, a wet washcloth in front of my face. "Here," Damon said.

I got his soft voice again.

And it calmed my stomach in a way the puking hadn't.

"Thanks," I murmured, taking it. Shit, I shouldn't have had that catered lunch. I'd thought the salad had tasted off.

He sat on the edge of the tub. "You okay?"

I nodded. "Yeah. Just a long week."

Fingers brushed over my forehead. "You don't feel warm."

"I'm fine," I said, sitting back and wiping my mouth with the washcloth. The nausea had disappeared. "I think that I'd better lay off the extra pepperoni tonight though."

"Seems fair," he murmured. "I'll go put it in the fridge and get you a glass of water. Hang tight until I get back, okay?"

"I'm fine—" I began.

"You're tired and you just lost what little you've eaten of dinner." He placed a hand on my shoulder, lightly pressed me down. "Stay put. Clearly, your body has had enough."

I debated arguing with that.

But then fatigue swept through me again, and I was reminded again of the long week and Grant and just felt really, really tired. Maybe we could have our weekly night with me prone on the couch.

I closed my eyes, leaning forward and rested my forehead against the cool porcelain.

Gross, but at least I'd just cleaned the bathroom.

Lie, my housecleaner had come in that day and cleaned . . . because I was *that* person. But I was also a person who traveled a lot and worked fourteen-hour days and was glad to have the means to be puking into a clean toilet.

"All right, ready to get up?"

I nodded but didn't move. I was just going to close my eyes and go to sleep right . . . now—

Damon lifted me up into his arms.

"Here, baby," he murmured. "I'll take you to bed—"

"No!"

He froze, fingers brushing my cheek. "I'm not going to—"

"Just couch, Damon. Okay?"

"Eden."

Just Eden. Not sharp but soft. Waiting and patient until I opened my eyes and stared up at him.

"I won't," he murmured.

I sucked in a breath. "I know," I murmured back. "But I need this. Tonight. Can we just watch something lousy on Netflix and be lazy?"

Warm chocolate eyes. "Minus the pizza?"

"And the garlic bread."

"Okay, love," he said with a nod. "We can do that."

And then he carried me over to the couch, setting me as gently on it as he might handle one of his very expensive cameras. He grabbed a blanket from the end, tucked it over me, then sat on the floor by my shoulder and reached for the remote. "So, what are we watching? Reality TV or a cheesy movie?"

My eyes were drifting closed already. *"You've Got Mail."*

"That's not cheesy, love," he murmured.

"I know." My words were slow, lazy. "But it's got daisies." A beat as I yawned. "And I love daisies."

Silence, then a soft, "Good to know."

He cued the movie up, hit play.

"And books," I whispered.

Damon turned his head. "It does."

"And a happy ending," I murmured, giving up the battle

with fatigue and letting my lids close and the intro of the movie wash over me.

I was so close to sleep that I nearly missed Damon whisper, "You can have one, too."

But I did hear it.

Though before I could feel panic at the words, sleep had tucked its talons into me and fully pulled me under.

And when my alarm woke me up in the morning, though I hadn't set it, and I found myself tucked safely in my bed, a glass of water on my nightstand. I knew Damon had stayed to make sure I was okay.

I was also glad I'd moved past locking the bedroom door.

I was even more glad for the coffee, brewed and ready to go in the kitchen, and the scrawled note telling me he hoped I felt better.

But, and I wasn't admitting this, even to myself, I also missed that Damon wasn't there himself.

Shit.

I was screwed.

So freaking screwed.

A week later, I struggled with the dress, the material bunching and having gotten stuck on my hips.

Cute.

My wrestling with the skintight nylon should have been a scene *in* the rom-com I was shooting with Grant. No doubt, it was hilarious watching me shimmy and wiggle and then sigh in defeat, arms flapping to my side.

So, the knock at my door wasn't welcome.

I yanked at the straps, trying desperately for a few more seconds to get it up and over my breasts, but then the knock came again, and I figured that at least half of the set had already seen me in my skivvies and so it wasn't much different for me to answer the door in a bra and half a dress.

I pushed it open and froze.

Damon.

Standing outside my trailer door with a pizza box in his hands. "Hey," he said, words coming fast. "You'd said it was okay to visit you on set, and I thought since it was Thursday Pizza Night that I'd—"

He broke off his speech, eyes widening.

"I'm stuck," I said, rather helpfully, I thought.

His throat working as he swallowed. "Um, I see that." He coughed. "Should I wait out here? Or get someone to help?"

I smiled at the thought of Damon running around set, declaring a fashion emergency. "No," I said. "I'm sure I can get it. Come in and have a seat. Pizza sounds perfect. I still have an hour before call time."

He followed me into the trailer, making himself at home on the couch before I slipped back into the bedroom area to continue my acrobatics with my dress.

But after a couple more minutes, I hadn't made much progress.

I was going to have to send Damon on the fashion emergency run after all.

A knock on the wall.

"Can I help?"

Honey and velvet. Goose bumps lifting on my nape, heat sliding slowly down my spine, moisture pooling between my thighs . . . fear making my pulse speed up. Or maybe that was longing?

Because I couldn't—

"Ed? Want me to try?"

Fuck. Yes, I needed help and I needed it from Damon, so

now wasn't the time to be a wuss. *No. Be smart. Don't get attached or let him close or make ties—*

"Okay," I whispered.

A beat then soft footfalls coming my way, heat soaking into the exposed skin on my spine, spice teasing my nose . . . fingers on my waist.

I shivered.

"Cold?"

It was a husky question, one that had any words drying up on the tip of my tongue. Instead, I mutely shook my head, holding perfectly still as one of his fingers trailed along my skin.

"You've made quite a mess of this."

I cleared my throat, forced my mind to focus. "Yup. It's a skill of mine. Making messes of things."

I'd meant . . . hell, I didn't *know* what I meant, but I know what my words made us both think of.

That morning.

The kitchen table.

And the mess—the glorious, pleasurable, most wonderful mess I'd ever been part of making.

I coughed. "Well anyway, I'm also really good at not being able to squeeze into insanely tight dresses when I've indulged into a few too many Pizza Nights."

Damon cleared his throat, the damp heat of his mouth caressing my shoulder blades. "Should I go put the pizza on the craft services table when we've gotten you unstuck?"

I pouted. "God, no. Why would you suggest giving away perfectly good pizza?"

"Well, you said the dress was tight, and I know you have to work for a few more hours," he said. "I thought you might not want a stomach full of heavy food, especially when you have to be on camera."

"I need fuel to keep working." A grin. "And I'm done with

starving myself to look good on film," I said, proud my voice was steady. "I'm not saying I don't want to be healthy or feel good, but if I can't have pizza and garlic bread once a week and still be successful in this industry, then I don't want this job."

His fingers had been working on the tangle on my right hip, but at my words, they stopped.

I kept talking. "I have enough money put away from my modeling days that I'm pretty set. I can afford to be choosy. I can afford to be myself." A shrug. "Sorry, apparently I'm feeling very life coach-like today. I just mean that—"

"I think what you said is exactly why you will be successful in this industry, Eden," he murmured. "It's why I've liked you so much from the beginning. You're *you*, always. Sometimes that's gentle and sweet, sometimes that's vulnerable, sometimes that's tough and fiery. But it's always real. No pretense. No shields—"

I snorted. "Oh, I've got shields, Damon. I think you, for one, can speak to how thick they are."

"Armor isn't the same as a shield."

That made me shake my head. "That doesn't make any sense."

He sighed, tugging up the tangle of fabric before moving to work on my left side, but he stepped around to my front as he did so, chocolate eyes coming up to meet my green ones.

Mint chocolate chip.

The perfect combination of ice cream. Maybe it could be perfect in us—

"I say that armor and shields are different because shields are raised to ward danger off. They're strong and heavy and can only be held up for a limited amount of time," he said, freeing an inch of the fabric. "But armor is different. It's donned and worn through battle. It's heavy like a shield, but it's not easy to lay down. Knights had people to help them take it off."

I sucked in a breath.

He shifted slightly, chest inches from mine, head bent, eyes locked on the tangle, but the angle meant that his mouth was very close to mine. "Armor needs help to be removed," he said softly, "but that help has to be earned, to be provided by someone the knight trusts. A shield, they can let fall to the ground without assistance."

"Are you saying I have a shield or armor?" I asked, and yes, it was breathless.

But Damon wasn't breathing steady either.

"I'm saying you have both," he murmured. "But that you've never been afraid to lay down your shield, to take those blows . . . because your armor is so strong, nothing can touch that inner core of you."

My breath rattled out between my lips, my heart pounding as I absorbed the words, absorbed the truth to them. Part of me had always been willing or able to make that bodily sacrifice, just to protect the sliver of hope that better things were ahead that had managed to persist deep inside my heart. I had sacrificed my body when my husband hurt me, when my parents used an outdated and horrible law to marry me off.

Then I'd sacrificed my body to make money, to provide myself a future. I'd dropped the shield a lot, the fear of using my body as fodder having long faded away as the necessity to eat and have a safe place to live ruled. But all the while, the armor surrounding that hope got stronger and heavier.

Damon succeeded in freeing the last tangle, tugging the fabric up, helping me slip it over my arms and onto my shoulders. He hadn't spoken as I'd been lost in thought, more proof that he knew me, had come to know me over many years.

He slipped around to my back, smoothing the dress before tugging the zipper up, still quiet, still working it out.

"You seem to be able to get underneath it."

His fingers had been between my shoulder blades, still

clutching the tag at the top of the zipper, but my words made him freeze.

"What?"

A sharp whip of a word.

I turned, knocking his hands away in the process. "*You*, Damon. You've taken years to earn my trust. You've been patient and kind and *my friend*." I cupped his cheek. "It's why you're under my armor."

"Your friend?"

My breath caught.

That was a loaded question. One I couldn't answer. I might have survived something horrible. I might have realized that Damon was there, deep inside, but I realized in that moment, that I still had hope, and it was safely tucked away.

To expose it to the elements, even if those elements included someone like Damon, was too much, too soon.

"Yeah," I whispered. "Your friend."

I think that if I hadn't been facing him, hadn't been so close, hadn't been staring directly into his eyes, I would have missed it. I wouldn't have seen the hope in his eyes wither and die, wouldn't have felt my own hope, locked up so tightly, pulse in sympathetic pain.

But then he smiled and stepped back, my hand cupping his cheek falling to my side. "All set," he said. "I'll get our pizza ready so you can eat before your call time."

One more searching look, one more moment of his eyes filled with disappointment before he turned and started to walk back to the front of the trailer.

"Damon?"

He paused, glanced back over his shoulder.

I bit my lip, wanting to say so many things but not knowing how. "Um . . . thanks." A beat. "Thanks for being my friend."

"No problem, sweet—" He shook his head. "No problem, Eden. I'll always want to be your friend."

Sweetheart.

He'd bitten back a *sweetheart.*

That hurt almost as much as him saying he wanted to be my friend.

And yet, I had no one to blame but myself.

Damn.

NINE

Damon

FRIENDS.

Fuck.

I tossed pizza onto the plates, my fingertips burning from having touched her skin, my hands aching from having resisted the urge to tug her close to my body, my mouth watering from the desire to slant my lips across hers.

But friends.

But . . . not giving up.

Remember?

I sighed, shoved down the disappointment that came from being called a friend, even after all the effort I'd put into being something more, and reminded myself that I'd promised patience and perseverance.

She was worth it.

I'd find a way through all that heavy armor. I had to.

You seem to be able to get underneath it.

Yeah, that.

I needed to remember what she'd told me, that it was a huge

step, and major progress. It was natural she would feel vulnerable about it, that she would then retreat after making an admission that put herself out there.

But progress. I just needed to set my ego aside enough to remember it.

Eden came out of the back, her footsteps shaking the trailer slightly as she moved. Keeping my attention firmly on her face, I tried to judge for myself if indeed I'd truly made it under that armor. But her emerald eyes held no secrets that I could deduce.

She'd picked up the shield.

Hey dumbass, you just pointed out she'd reached out and because of that, she was going to retreat. Of course, she picked the shield back up.

Good times that I was now having mental arguments with myself.

That was the surest sign of stability.

Snorting to myself, I picked up a plate, along with a handful of napkins, and turned to hand them to her, still focused on her face, still rather pointlessly trying to figure out what was going on in her brain. Though, maybe that wasn't the stupidest thing I'd been doing of late, the least of which was bringing her greasy pizza when she was due on set in a few.

The biggest of which was faking a date in order to think that she might care enough that I was going out with another woman.

Her response to that had been lukewarm—I thought I'd detected a little disappointment in her texts, though they were texts and context was hard to fully grasp, but when I'd stepped back a little, hoping she would reach out, she hadn't. And then the next week's Pizza Night had been perfectly friendly.

Friendly.

If one could consider throwing up and then passing out, *friendly*.

Ugh. I was definitely beginning to hate that word.

I stifled a sigh, put the second-guessing about whether I was playing this situation right aside, and just focused on the moment. I was with Eden. That needed to be enough.

"When are you due to hair and makeup?" I asked, and I'd been so focused on her face, on my own inner monologue, and the stupid fucking pizza, that I hadn't fully processed what she was wearing.

A fucking doozy it was.

Or maybe a two-by-four to the temple.

Because *that* dress.

I'd known it was red.

I'd known it was tight.

I hadn't been able to fully predict the effect a garment could have on me. I should have known—it was kind of what I did for a living, capturing the best angle, the best light and shadows, the most visually satisfying expression of the individual being photographed.

But this wasn't any of that.

It was Eden, which was a gut punch on any day.

But Eden in *this* dress.

Holy fucking shit, it was a miracle I had an ounce of sense left and managed to return my gaze to her face. I really, *really* enjoyed the mental survey I took on the way. Long legs, short skirt, flared hips, and breasts . . . good God, had her breasts always been that big?

Fuck. I was turning into a pervert.

Except, *God,* I wanted to get my mouth on them.

I needed—

She sat down next to me and took a bite of the pizza, talking around it. "I've got about twenty minutes. It won't take long," she said. "They'll just touch up what I've got going here."

"You look beautiful."

Green eyes on mine. A shy smile on her lips. "Thanks." Another few bites then she added, "Of course, that won't help much. We're shooting the rain scene. Which means this pretty dress"—she brushed a hand down her side—"is about to get doused with water."

Pebbled nipples.

See-through fabric.

Okay, so the last one was probably unrealistic considering the color of said dress, but a man could hope, couldn't he?

The first, though . . . yeah that was going to be in my fantasies for life.

My cock twitched, I cleared my throat, and fuck, but the image of water sluicing down her skin brought me right back to that day at her house, the kitchen table, the syrup and sugar, then washing it off afterward.

Maple-scented hair, silky skin—

So not helping my dick-twitching situation.

I needed to pull it together and—

"Do you still have that shoot this weekend?"

I nodded absently, picking up the pizza from my plate, mainly to shove something in my mouth so I wouldn't say everything I was thinking. Which was basically, 'Get naked and I'll bend you over this couch.'

That was not patient, nor friendly.

So I shoved a giant bite into my mouth and just nodded at her question.

"I thought you weren't working for a few months."

I shrugged, chewing for several long minutes before I was able to swallow the hunk of a piece I'd taken. "It's been a couple months."

"No, Damon," she said. "It's been *one* month."

"Nope." I shook my head. "It's been seven weeks since I

finished my last job and came home. So I'm technically on month two, which means it's been a couple."

She rolled her eyes. "That's hardly logic."

"It's photographer logic," I said, setting my plate down and leaning back. "Which means it's solid gold."

A snort. "Solid gold shit." Wrinkling her nose, she set her plate down. I noticed she'd barely eaten anything.

"Are you okay?"

Lips pressed flat, she rubbed her stomach lightly. "Yeah, I think my dress is too tight for pizza consumption."

"I hadn't noticed."

She grinned. "Stop trying to be charming. I'm imitating sausage at this point."

"I said it once and I'll say it again, you're beautiful."

"I'd be a lot more beautiful if I didn't feel like I was going to upchuck." She stood and stretched her back with a soft groan. "How am I supposed to look like I'm longingly searching for my long-lost love while depressingly walking through the rain, all while looking sexy?"

"I'm not sure even Meryl Streep could pull that off."

Another wrinkle of her nose. "I don't think a little nausea would slow down Meryl."

"I—"

I stopped, my brain pinging with a warning. Last week, with the vomiting, tonight with the nausea. This tight dress. The breasts I could swear were bigger.

The fact that I'd used a condom during our night together.

But . . . had I used one in the kitchen?

I had to have. I'd never not used one. I always took extra precautions and—

"Was the dress always this tight?" I blurted.

Say yes, say yes—

"Um . . ." She frowned, eyes drifting to the side as she

considered my question. "No? I guess it wasn't quite *this* tight during fittings. I mean, it was definitely restrictive, it has this built-in corset thing that squeezes and lifts . . . well, anyway Pizza Night is catching up with me. I'll just have to cut back."

"Are you—" I broke off, not sure how to phrase it. "I—"

Shit.

I shouldn't do this now. If she wasn't worried about possibly being pregnant because my dumb ass hadn't used a condom that morning, then the best time to give her that bit of information wasn't right before she had to go and film the most pivotal scene in the movie.

"Damon?"

She'd been pacing back and forth, bare feet padding almost silently across the floor. Now, she'd stopped and looked at me.

Because I was being really fucking weird.

Really weird.

Shit. I needed to not panic. I needed to not panic *her*. Not when I didn't know for sure and when she was working.

I forced a smile, popped to my feet. "Sorry, I'm . . . uh . . . I just had the best idea for the shoot. I'm going to take off, so I have time to try it before the sun fully sets. I'll leave the pizza—"

"Dam—"

"Can I bring you breakfast tomorrow?"

"I—"

I reached for the door handle, pausing to look back. "French toast?"

She froze, face freezing.

Shit. Not French toast. I needed to suggest something else. Omelets? Burritos? *Fuck*. Who gave a shit about breakfast? All I could think was that she'd had her big break, her career was just taking off, and I'd impregnated her—

A shake of her head, her frozen expression clearing away. "French toast sounds perfect. Ten?"

"Ten," I agreed.

Then I pushed open the door and I got the fuck out of there before I said something that might ruin her night, her scene, her life . . .

Something *else* that was.

TEN

Eden

I'D SLEPT a solid eight hours, but I was still exhausted when I crawled out of bed at a quarter of ten the next morning.

Shooting had run until well after midnight, but my driver had gotten me home immediately after we'd wrapped. Which meant I'd been tucked into bed by just after one. Not the latest I'd been up, not by a long shot, but paired with all the long days of filming, and probably more likely, dealing with the emotional exhaustion that was Grant, and I was more tired this morning than any other time I could remember in recent memory.

But breakfast was being delivered by the wonderful Damon, and I had two whole days off from shooting.

We'd pick up on Sunday, push through the final weeks of filming in New Mexico, and I'd be done with Grant.

Until promotion.

Joy of joys.

But that wasn't scheduled until next year, and so I had a full three-hundred and sixty-five days to recover.

Sometimes I had to focus on the simple things in life.

Snorting, I turned on the shower and spent the next ten minutes washing off the fatigue—though not my hair. Not only did I not have forty-five minutes to dry it, but throughout filming, my locks had been washed, dried, curled, and teased too many times over—not to mention slathered with products and also food from the dinner-gone-wrong scene. They'd also had slime in them along with artificial paint.

Basically, my hair had been put through the wringer and it needed a break.

So I tied it up, dry shampooed it, and then tugged on leggings and a cozy sweater.

I'd give it some quality attention later. A conditioning mask would go a long way toward rehabbing my working girl hair.

No makeup, because clearly, my face had undergone as much on the makeup front as my hair had on the styling front.

Luckily, Damon wanted to be just friends.

I sniffed. So, he didn't need to see me dolled up.

Of course, I was also deliberately ignoring the fact that I'd been the one who wanted to stay just friends, that he'd wanted to continue on that day, that he'd stuck around since then.

I'd just thought—

"What?" I said, glaring at myself in the mirror. "I'd say he got in under the armor, nearly have a heart attack from admitting it, and then he'd tug me into his arms and declare his unending love? And I would just be magically okay with that?"

First, I didn't think I wanted that. Okay, that was a lie. A part of me *did* want it, but the rest of me couldn't fathom a world where I just put the past behind, jumped on the HEA bandwagon, and galloped down the aisle.

Even if that person was Damon.

Because, second, I couldn't let someone in. I *physically* didn't think I could do it.

Although . . . and this was the third point, Damon was *already* in.

My heart skipped a beat at the thought, throat tightening, fear shivering down my spine.

"Stupid," I muttered.

I met my gaze in the mirror again and saw the truth within them. I'd stood in front of a mirror like this many times before. Sometimes, like now, my green eyes filled with fear, sometimes they were ringed in black eyes, sometimes they were judging or assessing as I did my makeup or prepared to do a photoshoot or walk the runway. But many more times I stood like this, emerald depths empty, my emotions shoved down and locked away.

Not anymore.

The edge of the Band-Aid had been peeled up slowly, millimeter by agonizing millimeter. First, by the photoshoot six years ago followed by the weekly calls, then by Artie and Pierce and filming *Carrot*, then Daphne and her sweet, newborn innocence . . . and then Damon in my bed, Damon at my house, Damon in my trailer.

Damon making me feel.

Damon—

Enough.

I yanked open the drawer on my vanity, knowing that even if I wasn't going to wear a bunch of makeup for him, that I'd still need moisturizer. The dry air in California demanded it. Except . . . the bottle wasn't on my counter. My eyes searched the drawer's contents, then the countertop. I didn't appear to have slung it either place while washing my face half-asleep the night before.

"Damn," I muttered, bending to pull open the cabinets. Not there. Not there. Not—

I spotted it on my dresser in the closet.

Right next to the hamper.

Thank God it hadn't made it inside. That would have been a mess, not to mention a waste of a very expensive moisturizer if it had taken a ride through the washer-dryer.

Delirious. Clearly, I'd been delirious last night.

Glancing at my phone, I saw it was only a few minutes before Damon was due to arrive. I hurried to the closet, snagged the bottle, and whipped back around toward the bathroom—

"*Ouch!*"

I'd slammed my elbow into the shelves that were in one corner, knocking a small box off the top, where I'd stashed it.

Stashed it out of sight.

Because it was *that* box.

The small cardboard shoebox hit the carpet, its lid falling off, contents spewing everywhere—a bit of lace, a narrow gold band, a picture of me and Tim, my eyes bright and excited, Tim's already lined with rage that would become physical pain for me. A dried rose and another picture, this one a smaller black and white image that had been beyond precious.

I stared at the picture and . . . the pieces in my mind shifted and realigned.

I'd already lost everything.

That little rectangle had once been critically important to me . . . and I'd lost it.

The doorbell rang.

Damon was here.

My lungs froze, breath locked inside. Then a sob escaped.

"F-fuck," I stuttered. I didn't want to lose *him*, too. I *couldn't*. I didn't want to be alone.

No.

I didn't want to be alone if that meant I wouldn't have Damon, if I just let the connection I had with him fade away. For him to find a future with someone else while I was left behind, still stuck in the same pattern I was now, living a half-life, wanting more but too scared to go for it.

Because Damon was different.

He'd always been soft where Tim had been sharp and brutal. He was supportive and kind, a thoughtful friend, a lover who was more focused on my pleasure than his own.

All that was without me giving him anything in return.

Patience when I'd only offered the opposite.

Damon wasn't Tim, and I wasn't the same woman with him as I'd been with Tim. I was more and stronger and healthier and, *dammit*, I deserved to find my only little slice of a happy future.

And I wanted to have that future to include Damon.

The fear gripping me for so long began to slowly disappear, replaced by tiny bubbles of hope, sneaking out from the seams of my armor. Maybe . . . I could have Damon without him having power over me? Maybe, we could build something where I didn't need to constantly be picking up my shield and donning my armor? Maybe—

The doorbell rang again.

Maybe, I needed to stop musing about the past, open up the front door, and take a chance.

Could I?

I glanced down at the black and white picture and thought, *How can I not?*

I stowed the items back in the box, putting it on the shelf, though not shoving it onto the top one this time.

No more shame. No more of my past holding me back.

I walked out of the bathroom, pausing to glance at myself in the mirror again, half-expecting my face to have undergone a complete change after what I'd worked through in the past five minutes.

But I was still just me.

Green eyes, red hair, pale skin—

My cell buzzed and I glanced down, saw that Damon had sent me a selfie of him wearing a sad face and holding up a bag of food from my porch.

I grinned then sucked in and released a long, slow breath. I could do this.

Sorry. Was in the shower. The code to the garage is 6262 if you want to let yourself in.

A beat.

And now you'll never get rid of me. *insert evil laughter here*

I sucked in another of those breaths. Just go for it.

Keep bribing me with sugary carbs and I'll consider it.

I hit send before I really considered what I wrote, and when I saw those words on my cell's screen, I couldn't believe that my fingers had typed them. *I'll consider it?* Holy fucking shit. My hands shook as I set my phone down, chest heaving, panic rising again—

Dammit.

"Just *enough.*"

Cold water splashed on my face, hair pulled back into a tight ponytail, clothes straightened and free of wrinkles.

And it *was* enough.

To snap out of this cycle, to accept Damon wasn't my ex. That I was different with him than I'd been with Tim. That I was different *now.* I'd pushed through the nightmare, had let it lead me to a new life and a new future. That was great and showed I was strong, that I could persevere, but—

I sighed. But if I pulled back now, had I really moved beyond the past?

No, because if I didn't do that with *all* parts of my life, then it didn't mean anything. If I was too scared to even consider that I might be able to build a future with a loving partner, with someone like Damon, then I had no hope of doing it with anyone.

But . . . I *had*. I was already breaking through that wall, *wanting* more.

And I was starting to think that I'd put so much effort into pushing Damon away in the first place, specifically because I knew deep down that he was different, knew he had the ability to get inside my armor.

"He *is* different," I whispered to myself, ignoring my wide green eyes. "He's *everything.*"

My heart skipped a beat, but I nodded and stepped back from the counter.

No more dithering. I was doing this.

"Eden?" Damon called, his voice slightly muffled. "Everything okay?"

Was it?

I glanced in the mirror, nodded once more, though more firmly this time.

Everything was going to be just fine.

I strode out of the bathroom, pushed through the open doorway, and spotted Damon at the end of the hall.

Not thinking. Not this time.

Not stopping. Not this time.

I ran toward him and launched myself into his arms. The containers in his hands hit the floor, food exploding everywhere, but I didn't pay any more attention to that than I would have a gentle breeze. It was Damon I was focused on, Damon I needed more than anything, Damon—

Whose lips were soft, whose body was hard, who . . . kissed me like I was the most precious object in the universe before gently separating his mouth from mine.

"Eden, baby," he said softly, his lips curved, chocolate eyes warm. "You've made a mess of breakfast again."

Clink. A big piece of the armor I wore fell to the floor.

I was surprised the sound didn't reverberate through the house, it felt so monumental inside my soul, but . . . Damon didn't appear to notice. He just hefted me into his arms, stepped carefully over the mess I'd made by knocking the food from his hands, and carried me into the kitchen.

"What do you have against breakfast, baby?"

I laughed, nuzzled closer into his arms. "Apparently a lot." I giggled. "And here I always thought I loved French toast." He started to carry me to the table. "Hey, wait. Put me down. I should go clean up the mess and then cook you something."

He kept walking. "I've got it."

"Dam—"

"I've got it." He set me down.

I started to stand, but he crouched down in front of me and rested his hands on my knees. "I've *got* it."

My heart swelled. "Okay," I whispered.

He nodded, stood, and crossed to the little closet where I kept my cleaning supplies. I waited as he gathered paper towels, a bottle of cleaner, and the trash can, but the moment he'd disappeared back into the hall, I pushed to my feet and began raiding the fridge. I might be tired and have just decided to take a terrifying step forward, but I could still make a mean batch of blueberry pancakes.

And bacon.

Mmm.

I reached for the package in the meat drawer. Yes, we definitely also needed bacon.

I brought it out, set it on the counter, and began measuring ingredients. Flour and baking soda, a dash of salt, milk, oil, eggs. I'd perfected this recipe over the years and so in just a matter of minutes, I had a bowl filled with batter and was setting a pan on the burner to preheat.

"Stubborn."

Damon was behind me, leaning against the counter, cleaning supplies at his side, trash can by his crossed ankles.

I turned back to the stove. "I ruined breakfast, so the least of what I can do is make you some of my famous pancakes."

"Famous how?"

I flashed him a grin over my shoulder. "Famous because they're the one thing that I can cook."

"What about your guacamole?" he said. "I can speak from experience that it's delicious."

"First, guacamole isn't an acceptable breakfast food—"

"Says who?"

I snorted. "Second, chopping things up and throwing them into a bowl isn't cooking."

A beat then the packet of bacon was snatched from my hands.

"Hey!"

"If you can't cook, then I'd better save this bacon from your hands." He smirked. "Also, I think chopping things up and throwing them into a bowl is the definition of cooking."

"I—" My words faltered when he came very close. "Okay, fine. That's reasonable."

He nodded.

Then we worked side-by-side in silence for a few minutes, him putting the slices of bacon onto the pan, me giving one more mix to the batter before ladling it onto the griddle.

"We going to talk about that kiss?" he murmured.

I bit my lip, sucked in a breath, then just let it rip.

"That kiss was hopefully the start of more—" He sucked in a breath, but I put my hand onto his arm. I glanced up, saw his face had gone hopeful, and I felt a blip of panic. Then I thought about that black and white picture, the sonogram of the baby I'd lost, and I knew that I had to keep moving forward. "But no, I don't want to talk about it." His expression sobered.

"Instead, I'm going to tell you about my ex-husband."

ELEVEN

Damon

I NEARLY DROPPED the pack of bacon.

But I did manage to recover enough to set it on the counter, to turn off both burners, take Eden's hand, and tug her away from the hot stove.

She appeared to be warring with herself, one minute her face was open, the next it was filled with worry.

"It's okay," I assured. "You don't have to tell me—"

Green eyes glanced up to mine. "I realized something this morning . . ." A sigh, words trailing off.

I waited, giving her time to find her words, not wanting to rush her, even though she'd just dropped a pretty big bomb. Ex-husband? Eden had just turned twenty-eight, and I'd known her for six years now. She'd begun modeling a few years before I'd photographed her, so—

"I see you're doing mental math."

"I'm—"

A warm palm on my cheek. "It's okay." She smiled, but it didn't hide the pain in her eyes. "I—" A shake of her head.

"When I was a little girl, I dreamed about New York, about bright lights and being onstage. I dreamed about high heels clacking on sidewalks bustling with people. I dreamed that because it was as far away from my childhood as I could imagine." Her voice dropped. "And I dreamed it because I'd seen the show *Sex and the City* once at a friend's house who had cable. Because it seemed so bright and colorful and different from reality."

I carefully peeled her hand from my face then linked our fingers together. "What was reality?"

Eyes to her lap, shoulders lifting and falling on a breath.

Then she spoke, and it broke my heart.

"My parents were very religious," she said. "Which was fine. Growing up, I loved going to church, loved we could be social, that I could see my friends. When someone grows up in a rural community, any bit of social outing is exciting." Her lips curved up, but it wasn't a true smile. "I grew up in a small farming community in Kentucky, had to catch the bus at six just to get to school on time because all of the pickups were so far apart. It was the sticks. Some of my neighbors didn't have electricity or running water, though my house did. No TV though." Here her eyes warmed. "Hence, *Sex and the City* being so exciting."

I squeezed her hand lightly. "My sisters tell me it's important to any woman's education."

Eden laughed. "Yes, it was that."

Silence descended and I murmured, "You know you don't have to tell me anything, right?"

"But I do." She blinked rapidly. "I do because you need to understand why I feel the urge to retreat, why I've stopped any chance of some sort of deeper connection with a man before it ever had a chance to take root." A beat. "Except it didn't work with you. You wormed your way in, dug underneath my armor, and"—her lips tipped up—"generally made a nuisance of yourself."

"Ah," I teased lightly. "My mom's favorite joke."

She chuckled. "Have you always been a nuisance then?"

"Yup."

"Trouble." A squeeze of my fingers, her face growing serious once more. "I'm just going to blurt it out once and for all and be done with it."

I nodded.

She sucked in a breath and then she went for it.

"So, church was the thing to do. Wednesday, Friday, and Sunday night services, youth ministry on Saturdays, Bible study group on Tuesdays and Thursdays. I spent almost more time there than my own home. I definitely spent more time with Tim than my parents."

Tim.

Just hearing the way she said the name made my insides boil.

"Tim was a youth minister." She swallowed. "He had all of us girls coming to the church as much as possible, was grooming us, from what I understand now. But I didn't get it then. I just loved the attention, loved it when he focused it on me." A quick breath. "But he was also twenty-seven years older than my twelve when he first touched me sexually."

My jaw clenched convulsively.

Eden saw and lifted her palm, resting it there again. "It's okay," she said. "I'm okay now."

I bit back the urge to say that she abso-fucking-lutely was not *okay* based on what I'd seen just weeks before, but I didn't. This was her story, her time, her—

She noticed my inner war—of course she did—and her face softened.

"Oh, Damon." Her fingers flexed. "This is why."

"What is why?" I asked hoarsely, covered her hand.

"Because you care," she said. "Even though it happened years ago, you care."

"Of course, I care, baby," I told her. "The idea of you being hurt, being touched by anyone, but most especially by someone who was so much older, had so much power over you . . . *God*. I wish he was alive so I could kill him."

"Is it uncharitable for me to say I agree?"

"Fuck no, baby."

She smiled. "This is also why."

My heart skipped a beat, my stomach filled with butterflies. God, I loved this woman. I probably had for years, if I were being honest. Six years of staying in touch, six years of coaxing her to this moment.

Six long years that were worth it.

"I'm here," I said.

"I know." Another sigh. "So the last of it then, yeah?"

"If you want to share."

A nod. "The last of it. As you might have guessed, things progressed. Pretty soon I was sleeping with him and not surprisingly, since he didn't use protection, I got pregnant. I was thirteen. My parents freaked. The church freaked. *I* was freaked. But I loved Tim, or thought I did, anyway," she said. "So when they asked if I wanted to marry him, I agreed. I didn't want him to go to jail, like they said he would if I didn't. I didn't want to lose him."

My jaw was so tight that it actually throbbed, but I didn't interrupt.

"My parents consented, a local judge was paid off, and at thirteen . . . I was married." She shook her head. "We moved, obviously. The congregation was horrified and . . . Tim wanted to get me away from my family and friends. He wanted to isolate me, to control me." Her eyes closed. "And then he began hitting me. Often. For little things like not making his dinner taste good—no matter that I was thirteen and the most I'd ever cooked was pasta with butter or stovetop mac and cheese—or not folding his clothes correctly—I'd never even so much as turned on a washing machine. And for big things—like money being hard to come by and doctor's appointments being expensive. It started with smacks, then got harder, until he was breaking bones instead of just bruising skin. And eventually . . . he hit me hard enough to make me lose my baby."

"Oh, Eden." I tugged her into my arms.

"It was for the best," she said. "And I know that sounds callous, but if I'd brought up a child in that environment, if I'd exposed him or her to Tim, I-I don't know what would have happened. If he'd hurt my baby—" She rested her forehead on my shoulder. "I wouldn't have been able to forgive myself."

I held her tighter. "None of this was your fault."

"I know," she said. "Logically, I do. But . . . sometimes, I don't know how to move forward. I lost so much in so many ways, but worst was the feeling that the people who were supposed to love me hurt and abandoned me. Not just Tim, but my parents marrying me off to a pedophile and then never checking in on me." Her head came up. "They were ashamed of me, disappointed I'd been impure, and they turned away from me the moment the ink on the marriage license was dry. I heard nothing from them until I'd gotten my first big spread. And *then* they managed to find a way to be in touch."

Rage burned a fiery trail down my spine. "They wanted money?"

She nodded. "Apparently the tractor had broken down and the barn roof was leaking."

"You told them to fuck off, I hope."

"I gave them the money," she murmured. "And then made them promise to never contact me again. I was in New York. I was working. I was moving forward. I . . . didn't want to remember my past ever again."

"Oh, baby."

Her face was lined with exhaustion. "I know."

"I'm so sorry that happened to you."

"Me, too," she murmured. "But Tim managed to kill himself by driving his drunk ass into a tree, so there is some small amount of karma in this world."

"Well, couldn't have happened to a nicer guy," I muttered.

She froze and then she began shaking in my arms. For a second, I thought I'd made her cry, but then I heard the chuckles break free, the laughter escape. She leaned back, her green eyes glistening with tears, from the past or from the laughing, I didn't know.

"Thank you," she said, after taking a few deep breaths. "For listening, for understanding."

"Always," I murmured and then tugged her close again. "And I'm so sorry."

She hugged me tight. "I know. Because you're a good man."

We stayed like that, her pulled halfway out of her chair and into mine, our arms wrapped around one another, for long moments, but eventually she shifted, sitting back into her own chair. "Regardless, of everything, I'm glad I found my way to New York, even if it was from one very unrealistic TV episode."

I chuckled. "I'm glad, too."

"And for a long time, I thought pushing through my past meant not telling anyone, meant locking it up deep inside. Because of you, I know that I don't have to do that."

I shook my head. "No, baby. That's all you."

"I think I need to get on the actor bandwagon and see a therapist."

He brushed his lips to my temple. "I think you have the resources and so if you want to talk to someone, you should."

"Yeah." A sigh as she pressed her lips together, wiped a finger under each eye. "Okay. Enough sad. Let's eat pancakes and do nothing for the rest of the day." She stood then stopped, her face aghast. "Oh, no! What about your shoot? You said you had—"

"Done." I smiled. "It was with the sunrise. Just a few friends who wanted some maternity pics."

"You're getting to be quite the preggo photographer."

Speaking of . . . but shit, did I really want to bring up my suspicions after all she'd told me?

Fuck, no I didn't, but I *should* tell her as soon as possible.

Except . . . wouldn't she know? If she'd been pregnant before? Her boobs looked normal-sized this morning. I was probably worrying for nothing. It had been that incredible dress, lifting and emphasizing her *assets*. She didn't seem nauseated now, and that usually happen in the morning, right?

"Damon?"

I blinked.

Suspicions or not, I'd need to broach the topic.

Just not right now, not after the emotions of the morning.

Which was why I stood and slanted my mouth across hers, only pulling back when my lungs were screaming for oxygen, and cupped her cheek. "I think you promised me world-famous pancakes."

She grinned. "You'd better reciprocate with perfectly crispy bacon."

"I can do that."

Eden trailed me to the stove, scraping the ruined pancakes off the griddle and then turning it back on to reheat. "Damon?"

"Yeah?"

"You make me think that I can do a lot of things I never imagined possible."

Those words, more than anything Eden had said thus far

that morning, wove their way into my heart. I'd need them there because neither of us could have predicted the storm that was going to tear through the peaceful world we'd just begun to create for ourselves.

And I didn't mean the baby I suspected was growing in Eden's womb.

I meant something much darker, much more sinister.

And much more devastating.

TWELVE

Eden

"AND AFTER THAT, we've got some early PR stuff for the superhero flick—they want to get some promotional shots of you in your costumes, do an ensemble photo with the whole cast in theirs, and then want to film you doing some of those YouTube only features," Maggie said.

I lay back onto my couch, cell to my ear. "One of those Internet searches or quiz thingies?"

"Thingie is the technical term?" Maggie teased.

"Absolutely," I agreed.

"What's the matter?" Maggie asked. "What's that in your tone?"

"Nothing."

Well, nothing so much as the fact that Damon had filled my life with upheaval . . . or maybe not so much upheaval as *feelings*.

Yes, I was happy and hopeful.

Yes, I was also saying that as if it were a dirty four-letter word.

"Come on now," Maggie said. "You're my easiest client."

I grunted. "You always say that."

"So?"

"So what?"

"You know *what*."

"So, don't stop being it now?" I asked, lips quirking despite myself.

"Yes," Maggie said with a laugh. "Exactly that."

"I'm fine, Maggie," I said and sighed heavily. "I'm . . . um. I just— I guess—"

"You're scaring me."

"It's not bad," I reassured. "It's just that you might have to deal with some of those *Is Eden Pregnant?* stories."

"What?"

"I'm seeing someone new, like actually dating someone, and it's got me a little unsettled." I bit my lip. "Well, not unsettled, exactly. More excited, but also nervous." So much talk about pushing through the past and moving forward, but I couldn't even put what Damon and I were doing into proper sentences—

"*You're* seeing someone?" Maggie exclaimed. "As in, you, Eden Larsen, perpetual bachelorette and prime catch of the Hollywood elite has a *boyfriend?*"

I sighed and rolled my eyes, both at myself for not being able to find the words and for her, because she was as bad as me. "I *have* been seen with men before."

"And never more than *once*."

She had me there. "Maggie—"

"No judgment here," Maggie said. "It has certainly given me much less drama to deal with."

"Except for all of those articles accusing me of being a whore," I muttered.

"Pish. People have always had a problem with female sexuality." Maggie sighed. "That unfortunately doesn't seem to change. Too much sex and she's a whore. Too little and a prude. Too many boyfriends, not enough of them, too sexy of clothes, not sexy enough. I could go on and on, but it wouldn't make any difference. We're always going to be judged on what we do and don't do, but I don't want that stopping you from living your life."

"Even if it makes a shitstorm for you to clean up?"

Maggie snorted. "Are you planning on making a shitstorm for me to clean up?"

"Not planning on it."

"Good." A beat. "Now, who are you seeing?"

"Damon Garcia."

"The photographer?"

"One and the same."

"Honey and a silver bikini," she said with a cackle that had me chuckling. "So, that's the secret to getting a good man?"

"At least one that makes me smile and brings me pizza."

"Damn, girl, you did good."

I laughed outright. "I know I did."

"And . . . you're happy?"

Nodding, though she couldn't see me, I said, "I am."

"Good." A beat. "You know, if I was there right now, I'd hug you."

I grinned. "If you were here, I'd let you." A giggle. "Well, only if you could find a way to corral Grant's ego."

"I think that's impossible, Eden."

We both laughed. I said, "I think that's impossible, too," which set us both off again.

"Eden?" she asked when we'd eventually gotten ourselves under control.

"Yeah?"

"I'm happy that you're happy."

"I—"

"Sorry, I know I'm overstepping," Maggie said softly. "But I *am* truly happy for you, Ed. You work so hard and deserve to have someone in your life who appreciates you."

Friend.

I'd opened myself up, shed some armor, and . . . now I had Damon, and a friend—a real one, not just an acquaintance I was friendly with and not just an employee—in Maggie.

"Thanks," I murmured. "And feel free to overstep anytime. It's nice to have a friend."

Quiet then. "I agree. I've been in short supply of good ones of late."

Which is when I remembered her ex Ben. "Shit, I'm sorry," I said. "Here I've been going on and on about Damon and you and Ben—"

"First, you haven't been going on and on. You shared. You're happy. You deserve it and don't have to apologize," Maggie said firmly. "And also, just because my ex was an ass, doesn't mean that the people around me don't deserve their slice of happy."

"I—"

"And last, if I had a man like Damon Garcia interested in me, you'd better believe I'd give up my freedom and lock that shit down."

I giggled. "Are you saying I should put a ring on it?"

"Um. Yes. Absolutely, that."

I snorted. She giggled . . . then we both busted out laughing again. After a while, we managed to regain control and finished running through the final details of the publicity she'd scheduled me to do, then chatted about nothing for a few minutes more, before hanging up.

My cell had just hit the table when the knock on my trailer door came, the voice telling me they needed me back on set.

I sighed and sat up.

Back to the Ego. Joy of joys.

Still, at the end of the day I'd get to talk to Damon, and I found with that happy thought in the back of my mind, perhaps Grant didn't seem so terrible after all.

A lie.

But at least I had something to look forward to while I did my job.

That definitely made it less terrible.

"I—" Tally grunted as she struggled with the zipper on the back of my costume. "I just . . . there! I've got it!"

I patted my makeup artist's hand. "Thanks for the assist. That zipper is a bear."

"They've certainly got you poured in there. Can you even breathe?"

I sucked in a tentative breath. "Sort of?"

"Aw." Tally grinned. "The price of fashion and film."

"At least it's a fabulous dress if I'm suffering for both."

Tally laughed. "True." She turned to grab a brush and compact from the table. "Now, just one more touch up and you'll be ready to hit the New Mexico sun."

"And they said L.A. was hot."

A few strokes of the brush across my nose, my cheeks. "We *are* in the desert."

"Be logical, why don't you?" I muttered, smoothing my hands down my front. "Good thing this is the last scene for this dress. Any more and I'll be bursting out."

"You look beautiful."

"I *look* boobalicious."

A snort. "I wished that if my dress got too tight, it would only be in my chest region." The petite brunette patted her hips.

"This is where I always gain when I've had too many chocolates."

"Oh, believe me," I told her. "I've gained there, too. I'm just bloated, and I've indulged in far too many Pizza Nights of late." My smile was instant at the mention of pizza because it conjured up Damon. Damon, who'd spent the rest of the weekend at my house until I'd flown out on Sunday, who'd made me perfectly crispy bacon to go with my perfectly fluffy pancakes.

Who'd stayed even though I'd told him everything.

Who hadn't changed.

Who could order a mean DoorDash when it became clear that both of our cooking skills were limited to breakfast foods . . . or rather, one type of breakfast food for me (no, I still did not consider guacamole acceptable breakfast food), and two if you counted cinnamon-sugar toast and frying bacon for Damon.

And I'd run out of bacon.

I snorted.

"I'm loving that smile on your face right now."

My eyes drifted up, met Tally's mahogany ones. "I'm happy," I said simply.

"I'm glad," she said then grumbled. "One of us should be. I've got to go to Grant's trailer next. Sheila is *sick*—which basically means that she's had enough of his bullshit and so all of the rest of us are going to have to take a turn shouldering our fair share."

"I'm sorry."

"You've worked with him more than me."

"Except, he semi-behaves because I'm the *co-star*."

Tally snorted. "Sure, he does."

"Okay, he doesn't," I agreed. "But we're in the home stretch."

"Well"—she began gathering up her things—"I hope the man that made you smile like that keeps working his magic."

My lips tipped up at the mention of Damon and just that quickly, my mind drifted away from Grant and movie sets and tight dresses to how Damon had held me and slept in my bed, though we'd fallen asleep without making love both nights. Me, because I knew he was different, that *we* were different together and I didn't want to rush back into something and, him, well, I couldn't read his mind, but my guess was that he was being as patient as ever, waiting for me to show or tell him implicitly that I was ready.

But he *had* said goodbye early the previous morning with a kiss that had turned my bones to jelly or maybe cooked spaghetti or—

Lord, I was losing my mind.

"Yeah," Tally said, squeezing my shoulder. "Just like that." And then she slipped from the trailer.

I spent a few more minutes thinking about spaghetti legs and Jell-O before I followed Tally.

Though, I made a wide bypass of Grant's trailer on the way to set.

Despite that, I could still hear him complaining loud and clear.

Thank God I had Damon.

I was thinking the exact same thought later that week when I entered my trailer and discovered the pizza box on my table, the smell of cheese and tomato sauce filling the small space.

Thursday. Pizza Night.

God, I missed Damon.

Especially when I saw the pizza was heart-shaped.

Kicking my shoes off and grabbing my cell from my dresser, I called him. He picked up on the first ring, his soft, "Hey, baby," the best sound I'd heard all day.

"Hey," I murmured back. "Someone's setting high standards in the romance department."

He scoffed. "I just sent pizza."

"A heart-shaped pizza is in a whole other realm."

"Well, if you think that's impressive," he said, tone light. "You should see how I do flowers."

The image of a pizza shaped bouquet made me smile.

Hell, who was I kidding? I was *already* smiling. But thus was the power of Damon.

"How was the Ego today?"

I sighed and sank down onto the couch, thankful that Tally had caught me on the way back to the trailer and undid my zipper enough that I could actually breathe.

"That good, huh?"

"Mmm-hmm." My lips twitched as I leaned back against the cushions, letting my head tilt up toward the ceiling. I propped my feet onto the table and hit the speaker button. "Just one more day until I'm done with Grant."

"You've been amazingly patient."

"Unlike some persistent male who won't leave me alone."

"Unlike some persistent male who sends you pizza *and* a brownie."

I leaned forward, noticing the brown paper bag next to the pizza box for the first time. "Okay, I think I like the persistent male who sends me pizza and chocolate."

He laughed lightly. "Hit FaceTime, baby."

"Why?"

"I want to see your face."

"Ugh. No, that can't happen. I've been out in the sun all day. I've got sand in places you don't want to think about, and I think I'm sunburned . . . despite the fact that a crew member's job today was to hold an umbrella over my head anytime we weren't filming."

"It's the reflection off the sand," he murmured.

"Huh?"

"FaceTime, honey. I need to see that face."

I sighed but hit the button so video would connect us. It rang once and then his face was there, smiling gently out at me. I sniffed. "You have absolutely no right to look this handsome when I look like . . . *this*." I waved a hand down my dirty clothes.

"Why are you half-dressed?"

I moaned, reached for the brownie, and shoved a piece in my mouth. "Because I can't get out of this dress on my own. It's too tight." I ate another bite. "I need to get a Bowflex, or a Peloton or . . . to stop eating pizza." My laughter was almost delirious, but that was what four straight days of filming with Grant would do. "No, I can't do that. No matter how fat I get."

Something crossed Damon's face, an expression that I almost missed. But I couldn't pinpoint what it was—discomfort, fatigue, concern? "Well, I promise I'll like you whatever size you are," he said. "Now, what's this about a sunburn? How come they didn't give you sunscreen?"

Me trying to ferret out the expression faded as I giggled. "I don't think you noticed, bub, but I'm a redhead. My skin is so white it's almost translucent—"

"I like to think of it as white as vanilla ice cream." He did a chef's kiss. "My favorite."

I sat up, not because the description was inaccurate—it decidedly was—but because—

"Vanilla ice cream is your favorite?"

He shrugged, shifting positions for a moment before coming back with a slice of pizza. I was sticking with the brownie. I needed sweet carbs to self-medicate with after my day with Grant.

"Vanilla ice cream is delicious."

"On its own?" I finished off the brownie. "Like in a cup or on a cone?"

His lips tilted up. "Yes, Ed."

"Th-that's—"

"Vanilla is a perfectly acceptable choice for a flavor of ice cream."

"Yes," I agreed. "If it's melting over a brownie or piece of apple pie, or dolled up with chocolate sauce and sprinkles and whipped cream on a sundae. But on its own? Th-that's insanity."

I opened my eyes when he didn't reply, and saw that he was staring at me with a huge grin on his face. "I love that we always get onto the most random topics."

"There are hundreds of more interesting ice cream flavors than vanilla—mint chocolate chip, for example," I said. "Or cookie dough. Or double fudge brownie. Neapolitan, if you're really stuck on having vanilla, because at least then it's sandwiched by strawberry and chocolate."

"All great choices if you like chocolate." A beat. "Which I don't."

I sat up on a gasp. "You cannot be serious."

"Deadly."

"How did I not know this?" I asked, tapping my chin. "You think you know a man for years, and then he drops a bomb like *this* on you." I shook my head. "I don't know, Dam. I—this might be a deal-breaker."

He snorted. "You think you're so funny."

I grabbed a slice of pizza. "I know I'm funny. I'm the star of a rom-com, remember?"

Another snort. "And well on your way to Ego level."

My gasp was punctuated first by my giggle and second by me shoving pizza into my mouth. I'd been teasing about Pizza Night and eating till the cows came home, but in reality, I'd been sticking with vegetables, fruit, and low carb meals since I'd wrestled with my dress the previous morning.

Not starving, but throwing in a few healthy meals until I bounced back.

But I wasn't giving up my Pizza Nights with Damon . . . or my favorite clothes because I'd gotten too big to wear them.

And as a former model, I'd been given a few gems.

I wanted to be able to wear them again.

"Such a hypocrite," I murmured.

"Come again?" Damon asked, looking confused. Rightfully, too, since I'd been listening to him talk about his travels up to San Francisco. Apparently, he'd met up with a photographer friend, Tanner, and they'd gone out to dinner.

So, 'hypocrite' was way out in left field.

"Sorry," I said. "I was woolgathering. Not that I wasn't enjoying your story. I'm glad you caught up with your friend. It's me who was being a jerk and drifted off."

His eyes went warm. "What made you drift off?"

I waffled for a few seconds before deciding that I'd been truthful about this and so might as well be truthful about everything else. "Well, I *say* I'm not willing to sacrifice my happiness to be a certain size, and meanwhile, I don't want to get so fat that I can't wear my clothes."

There.

Right there.

That thing on his face again.

"Damon, what's going on? You've made a weird face twice tonight and—" Horror dawned and I dropped the pizza back into the box, appetite fading. "Is it about what I told you? About my ex? My family. I mean, I know it's a lot—"

"Eden."

"I know I'm messed up and—"

"Baby."

"I—"

"Eden."

Sharp. Unusual. Enough to snap me out of the spiral.

It should have reminded me of Tim, of my past, made me retreat, but even when Damon was sharp, he was still soft, if that made sense. Of course, like the rest of my mind this evening, it also didn't.

I . . . guess I just knew that Damon would do anything in his power to not hurt me.

And Tim hadn't cared.

"Yes?" I said, pulling myself out of my head.

"Nothing that happened to you in your first marriage was your fault," he said, fiercely. "None. Of. It."

"I know that."

"Do you?"

"I—" My rebuttal stopped. "I do," I whispered. "Or . . . part of me does, anyway."

"Yes, baby," he said. "It's the rest of you that keeps tugging you under."

"I hate that I can't forget."

"Maybe you need to stop worrying about forgetting and start seeing that your past has made you the strong, incredible, wonderful woman you've become today."

"I—"

I don't know what I was going to say because those words touched me so closely, so deeply that there wasn't any armor. Damon meant them—the sincerity was in every syllable.

"You make me think that's possible."

"Baby."

"I really like you," I whispered.

"Eden."

"You make me want more."

He sucked in a breath. "I think that's the best thing anyone has ever said to me."

"I'm going to try really hard not to screw us up."

A shake of his head. "We're both going to screw up, you know that, right?"

"If you say so," I murmured. "Because up to now, you've been pretty much perfect."

"Yeah?"

"Yeah."

His eyes danced with amusement. "Only pretty much?"

"Learn how to make French toast, and you'll be all the way there."

"Come up to San Francisco when you wrap," he said. "You can drive up with me to visit my folks. My mom makes the *best* French toast. But she's never given me the recipe. I bet if I bring you along, she'll cave and teach it to both of us."

"I—"

"No answer required right now."

"Damon—"

"It's okay," he said, sitting up. "I shouldn't push."

"Damon!"

He stopped talking.

"I was going to say that I'd love to go with you."

I was?

My heart began pounding in my chest, my throat went tight, my—

I was.

Moving forward, not forgetting, but not letting it define me. Not any longer. I deserved that. Damon deserved that . . . and I wanted it. I wanted a future with him.

"Baby."

I sniffed. "I know."

"I wish I could hold you right now."

"I wish you could, too."

We turned the conversation to lighter topics then—Damon dropping back into his story about Tanner and Tanner's fiancé Kelsey, and then telling me how he'd done some touristy things for the first time ever, including riding a cable car and getting ice cream at Ghirardelli's—vanilla, of course.

We hung up when I yawned three times in quick succession, and that meant that I never got to the bottom of the weird look on Damon's face.

Turned out, I only needed to use a little of his patience.

I was going to find out just after my plane landed in San Francisco.

And it was going to change absolutely everything.

THIRTEEN

Damon

SHE WAS the picture of Hollywood glamour, walking down the stairs of the private jet she'd hired, her jacket flowing behind her as she moved, red hair a shining sheet of fire down her back.

"Hey," she murmured, coming close and pressing a kiss to my lips, where I waited at my car, parked just outside the private tarmac.

"Hi, baby."

Her shoulders relaxed and she smiled up at me. "I've never let another man call me *baby*, you know that, right?"

"I'm special," I said with a sage nod.

"A special *something*," she teased.

"That much is true. Come on." I held open her door, waited until she was inside, then snagged her small suitcase from the attendant, slipping him some cash.

"Oh, no," the attendant began trying to give it back. "Ms. Larson already—"

"Keep it," I said. "You got her to me safely."

"I—"

I rounded the car and tugged on the driver's side handle. "Have a good night."

"Thank you." With a nod, he headed back to the plane.

"Everything okay?" Eden asked when I'd sat down and started the car.

"Everything's great," I said. "You're here. My parents aren't expecting us until tomorrow night, and I've booked us a hotel room in the city. We'll order room service and forget about the curse of the Ego."

"That sounds perfect."

I maneuvered us out of the lot and onto the freeway, glad I'd chosen a hotel that was close by. "*You're* perfect."

She smacked my arm lightly. "Stop being charming."

"It's all I've got."

"You've got a lot more than that," she said, and that she'd spoken the words in that tone, that she'd looked up at me like that—with warmth and truth and conviction —meant the world to me.

Damn. She absolutely slayed me.

"Baby."

"Shh," she said.

"I—"

"Just drive." Her hand dropped to my thigh. "I want to get to the hotel as soon as possible."

I didn't need the heat in her gaze to tell me what she wanted to do when we were there. Not when her desire burned through her tone.

Shit. I wanted that, but also, we needed to discuss my suspicions. "There's also something we should talk about—"

She leaned over the console and nipped my jaw. "Talk later. Fuck as soon as possible."

I should have told her the night before.

I should have told her the *week* before.

"I—"

"Later," she said firmly. "For now, just drive and tell me about your day."

I did what she asked. I drove. I told her about the day. I swallowed my guilt by telling myself that my suspicions about the state of her uterus were probably better served by a conversation that didn't take place in a moving vehicle.

But, in truth, it was avoidance, plain and simple.

We'd made such strides, and now I worried this potential unplanned pregnancy might cause the past to come flooding back into the present, might be the final straw.

That all the progress she'd made, that *we'd* made, would be undone.

Not for me.

I loved this woman, would take any hiccups in stride.

But Eden?

I worried she wouldn't be able to handle it.

And I was absolutely terrified that I was going to lose her.

"Mmm," she said, setting the bowl of soup to the side and picking up a piece of surprisingly good sushi.

I wouldn't have guessed a hotel's offerings would be so tasty, but this one's was.

She scarfed it down, doing a great job of out-eating me.

I was unsettled.

With a sigh, she dropped her hands to her stomach and rubbed it lightly. The action made my heart pulse, and I knew it made my face change because suddenly she bolted upright and exclaimed, "Oh no! Are you going to be sick?" She ran for the trash can and snagged it out from beneath the desk then rushed over and stuck it under my nose. "Do it in there. Was the fish bad?" She picked up the plate with the remaining sushi and sniffed. "It smells fine—"

"Eden."

She froze, head slowly rising so her eyes met mine. "That's a snap," she murmured. "On the first time."

I wasn't sure what that meant, but I set down the trash can and grasped her hand, tugging her so she sat on the bed next to me.

"Ooh, I like *this*," she murmured, crawling into my lap.

I'd managed to distract her from sex with food because her stomach had begun growling midway through the drive and hadn't stopped. Then I'd claimed I needed a shower and had hidden in the bathroom until the food had arrived.

Cowardly.

Ridiculous.

Which brought me to this moment.

"No, baby," I said. "I've been putting off bringing this up because I kept thinking there wasn't a right moment, that it might upset you, and—"

She leaned away from me, face going pale.

"It's not—"

I reached for her. She backed away.

I stood, hand out. "Please, come sit down," I said. "I need to tell you this. I can't go on without at least mentioning it."

Eden looked absolutely sick, but she nodded then sat back onto the edge of the bed. "Is what you're keeping from me why you've been so weird?"

Fuck. So much for sly.

"Yeah."

Her chin came up, her shoulders stiffened. "Fine. Just say it."

But, how to say this gently? How to break the news—

"I think you're pregnant," I blurted and forced my eyes to

meet hers, saw that her face was ashen, her eyes closed off, and I kept talking, the words coming faster and faster. "That time in the kitchen, I didn't use anything. I mean, I'm clean, but I have working sperm, at least I think I do. I've never tested it." I winced. *Shit. Move on, asshole.* "And . . . um . . . anyway you've been sick and nauseous, your clothes are tight, your boobs—" I flopped a hand in the direction of her chest. "They're—They've you mentioned they'd . . . grown. And I'm so sorry, I didn't even think about protection at the time and that was irresponsible." Another wince. "The possibility you might be pregnant didn't even occur to me until a week ago, and I've been thinking myself into circles, assuming one moment I'm wrong, because you'd know if you were and you wouldn't wait a week to tell me." I thrust a hand through my hair. "And then the next, I remember I didn't use a condom and the nausea and puking and boobs, and I think how could I have been so stupid? I—"

She put a hand up.

I shut my mouth.

"What the fuck, Damon?" She glanced down at herself. "I've only gained five pounds, and you think I'm pregnant. Do I look *that* horrible?"

Oh shit.

Oh. Shit.

"I've been indulging in pizza and set food and haven't been working out because of the hours I've been filming, but shit, it's only five pounds. Do I really look pregnant?"

Fuck.

I took a step toward her, hating the hurt on her face. "No, baby—"

"I have a narrow frame. A couple of pounds seems like a lot —" She sniffed.

"Eden. I wouldn't have even noticed if I hadn't realized about the condom—"

Her hand came up again, stopping me, and then the other came up, too, both of them cupping her breasts—which normally I would highly approve of. However, in this case, my cock was decidedly quiet.

Mostly because my stomach was churning from realizing I'd hurt her feelings.

"You think I'm fat," she whispered.

"No. Not at all. You're beautiful, baby," I said. "I just—the nausea, me being stupid enough to not use a condom— This is *my* fault."

"My boobs are bigger because I've gained weight over the last month." She touched her hips. "I've also gained here." She sighed. "My boobs are *extra* big this week because I just finished being on my period, and I always get swollen and a little extra busty during my time of the month. The puking is because I ate a catered lunch. I wasn't alone—half the crew got sick. The nausea . . . I think is a combo, the food, stress from dealing with Grant, my tight clothes, PMS."

"Oh."

She shook her head. "Yeah. *Oh.*"

"I'm sorry," I said, daring to take another step toward her. She didn't stop me, so I relaxed. Marginally. "I'm a total idiot."

"Not a *total* idiot," she muttered, her lips curving just the slightest bit. "I can see the signs you saw and why you thought that. I guess . . ." Another sigh. "My bigger concern is, why didn't you talk to me?"

"What?"

"You said you've known for a week. Why didn't you say something sooner?"

I hung my head. "You'd had that rough day with Grant before the Pizza Night in your trailer in L.A. and had to be back on set with him for that really important scene that night."

A nod. "And the rest of the time between then and now?"

"I didn't want to tell you on the phone."

"What about the weekend? We were together for two solid days and—"

"I was an ass," I admitted. "I was worried about your career and your projects, worried that we'd finally moved forward and were having such a great weekend. I didn't want to ruin that with . . ."

"Potentially life-changing information?"

Fuck.

I nodded, miserably.

"And if I'd decided to drown my Grant sorrows in a bottle or two of wine?"

"I would have . . ."

Hell, I didn't know what I would have done.

She stood, shook her head. "Damon."

"I know, baby. I should have just brought it up the moment I even thought it."

Eden moved toward the windows, staring out for several long moments. "I can't actually have kids, Damon," she murmured. "You should know that. I was . . . damaged when Tim pushed me down the stairs."

A knife-like blade of pain stabbed me in the heart.

"Baby," I murmured and stood.

She spun, put her hand up again.

"That's information you need, information you need to accept. I don't know if you want kids someday, but they can't be born of my body. Not anymore."

"Honey."

"If you want that, I can't give that to you."

"I just want you."

Tears trailed down her cheeks. "You say that now, but—"

No. I went to her, tugged her into my arms. "I've waited six years for a shot with you, Eden Larson. If kids are in our future, we'll find a way that works for both of us."

"I don't know if I'll ever get there."

I sucked in a breath, held her tighter. "You don't need to get *anywhere.*"

"And you still should have told me the moment you suspected." Her eyes locked onto mine. "You held back because you were worried I'd panic. That . . . we can't make a relationship of that."

"You're right."

"And if you *do* want them—"

"What I want is for us to enjoy our time together," I said, tucking a strand of her hair behind her ear. "And maybe figure out a way to get my mom to spill her beans on her secret French toast recipe."

She smiled. "I can do that." Then, "You should have told me."

"I know."

"We can't build something rock-steady if you hold back from me."

"I know that, too."

"I should be so fucking pissed at you right now. Especially since you thought I looked fat enough to be pregnant."

I winced, nodded. "Yes, you should."

She sighed. "Instead, I'm touched that you care about me so much that you didn't want to hurt me or my career."

My lungs froze.

She turned in the circle of my arms. "Thank you for caring, baby."

This woman. Fuck, she was absolutely incredible. I couldn't believe she wasn't roasting my balls over a fire, especially when I deserved a good searing. Instead, she'd set a boundary and forged a way forward.

And I knew I couldn't hold back.

Couldn't hold *anything* back.

Not ever again.

"I love you."

Her face froze, lips parting in surprise. But then she rose on tiptoe and pressed her lips lightly to mine.

"I love you, too," she said, shocking me, my jaw dropping open. Gently, she closed it and smiled up at me. "It's the only explanation."

I chuckled. "Besides insanity?"

Her smile turned full-grin. "Yes, exactly that," she said. "But also, Damon baby, it's the only explanation for why you were able to get inside my armor. It's love. It has to be because it's the only thing strong enough to penetrate all of that steel."

My heart expanded like a balloon being filled with helium. I started to wind my arms around her, but she leaned back, heels dropping to the floor, lips distancing from mine, eyes narrowing. "Now, there will be no stalling or hiding in the bathroom or acting weird," she said. "You're going to take me to bed, give me many orgasms in penance, and promise to never"—her fingers wove into the hair on my nape and gripped tightly enough to make me wince—"*ever* keep something like this from me again."

I scooped her up into my arms. "I promise."

"Good." Her hands fell to my shoulders. "Now, kiss me."

Another promise I could keep.

I dropped my lips to hers.

FOURTEEN

Eden

GOD. I loved his mouth.

His lips were soft against mine and yet demanding, coaxing me from touched, albeit mildly irritated, into heavy-limbed and flushed all over from desire by the time he'd set me down on the bed.

One moment to yank the comforter away.

Another and he was pressed down on top of me.

"Baby?" he murmured in my ear.

"Hmm?"

"You're sure?"

My eyes peeled open. "About the love thing or the orgasm thing?"

Damon brushed his finger down my cheek, the slightly calloused tip catching lightly against my skin. "Either. Both."

I did some tracing of my own, along the bristly edges of his jaw, down his nose, across his forehead, pushing several of the slightly overgrown brown locks out of the way.

"I'm sure about both." I leaned up to nip his jaw. "I'm also sure that you're way too handsome for your own good. You should have focused some of that Garcia Christmas Special magic in front of the camera."

He chuckled, shifting slightly so his mouth could reach my throat. "As sacrilegious as it seems to be bringing her up at a moment like this, my mother would love to hear you say that. She's always been on me to use my *connections* to get into movies."

I laughed. "Well, now you can use *my* connections."

A shudder. "God, no. The only connection of yours I want is finding a way into your pants."

How was this my life? I was lying in bed with a man who wasn't rushing to take off my clothes as quickly as possible, trying to find a way to his orgasm, to snag that moment of pure pleasure. But just as he wasn't racing to that end, I *also* wasn't hurrying. I'd spent so many of my sexual interactions since Tim searching to get lost in that moment of blissful oblivion, and disappointed when it only lasted a few seconds, when it didn't *mean* anything more than getting lost for a few seconds—

Empty oblivion.

I wanted more than that now.

I wanted to live.

I wanted to feel.

I wanted . . . Damon in my pants.

He nipped at my throat. "What are you grinning about?"

"You getting in my pants."

His head popped up. "Yeah?"

"Yeah," I said. "But you're sure taking your sweet time with it."

A wicked smile, heat in his eyes, his head dropping back down, and his mouth went to work. He traced his lips across my jaw, let them drift up to my earlobe, suckling gently. He'd discovered that spot the first time we'd been together, and it never failed to make me shiver and moan, goose bumps erupting on my arms.

"Mmm," I groaned, lacing my fingers into his hair.

He moved, shifting his weight, one hand sliding under the hem of my shirt, moving up along my stomach, between my breasts, up and down, up and down.

"Mouth," I demanded.

Damon didn't make me wait. His lips falling to mine, hand sliding out from beneath my shirt, and tugging at the buttons on its front, though not making much progress because it was one hand and he wasn't a magician.

I reached down to help him, our hands tangling as we both struggled with what I was mentally terming the devil's garment. Eventually, I batted him away, yanking open the line of them. I was so glad I'd taken matters into my own hands when his eyes darted up to meet mine for a moment, fire in their depths, before tracing slowly down the exposed skin.

"Now you," I whispered.

One flash of movement, one flex of those powerful arms, and his shirt was yanked up and over his head, disappearing somewhere over the edge of the bed.

"I—"

My chance for giving orders was over.

Damon's mouth dropped to mine for a long, hot kiss, then moved, over my cheek, down my throat, dancing over both collarbones, nudging my bra straps out of the way. His warm hand slipped beneath my back, flicked open the clasp and peeled the lace and cotton garment away, tossing it in the direction of his shirt.

"God, you have the most beautiful set of tits I've ever seen," he said, dropping his head and rubbing the bristles on his jaw lightly on the other side.

Normally, I hated the word *tits,* but there was something

about the gruff way he said it or maybe it was the roughness of his stubble raising goose bumps *not* on my arms, my nipples pebbling into tight, aching buds that made me not mind the word so much.

He sucked one of my nipples into his mouth, pinching the other lightly between his thumb and forefinger, making my back arch, my hips cant up in need.

And slow disappeared.

He switched sides and pleasure snaked down my spine, my thighs clenching together, moisture pooling between them. I gripped his head, torn between keeping his mouth there and dragging it back up to meet mine again.

In the end I did neither.

Because Damon was moving down my body, tongue leaving heated trails of moisture, teeth punctuating with little bites that made me jump and groan and grip his hair tighter.

Until my hands were extracted from his locks, and his went to work on the button of my slacks, sliding my zipper down, coaxing me to lift my hips so he could tug them down and off my legs.

They went the wayside, trailed quickly by my underwear and then I was naked, Damon shirtless as he crouched between my thighs.

"You, too," I repeated.

He grinned, that wicked one again that seemed to melt my bones from the inside out, but then he stood, fingers working at the button of his jeans for a heartbeat before they, too, hit the floor.

His boxer briefs stayed on for the moment, though he did reach for the pocket of his pants and pull out his wallet, along with the condom inside it, setting both on the bedside table.

Then he seemed to realize what he was doing and froze. "I'm—"

I reached for his hand. "Don't ever apologize for protecting me," I said. "Plus, the responsible thing is to use protection, even if I can't have a baby." I tugged him until he came back onto the bed. "I've never *not* used it. Or well, before you corrupted me."

He brushed a kiss to my lips. "I think you're the one doing the corrupting."

I batted my lashes innocently, totally ignoring the fact that I'd slid my hand down his front and was cupping him through the material of his boxers. "I don't know what you're talking about."

I squeezed.

He groaned, his hips jerking forward.

"So," I murmured, still cupping him. "Put it on. Or don't. But either way, just get inside me."

"Not quite yet." He slanted his mouth across mine, kissing me until my heart pounded, my lungs screamed for oxygen, and a sheen of sweat had broken out on my body. "Dam—" I began when he released my lips, but he only allowed me to suck in one short gasp of air before he was kissing me again, one hand coming to rest by my head, the other sliding down and slipping between my thighs.

He groaned again, the sound vibrating along my tongue, making me shudder and gasp . . . or maybe that was because his fingers had slid through the liquid dampening my pussy and then pushed inside.

A blunt invasion that definitely had me gasping, my lips tearing away from his, my head pressing back against the pillows, a long moan erupting.

"Mmm, baby," he murmured, shifting down, shoulder nudging my legs apart, mouth descending . . . to my belly button, to my hip, to the other . . . and then to my clit. "Oh fuck!" I gasped, pleasure exploding out from my center, filling me with fire. My hands somehow found their way to his hair again, tilting his head, grinding myself against his mouth and tongue, feeling the stubble abrade my sensitive skin, in a good way, in the *best* way.

No. That was his tongue. Or perhaps, the suction of his mouth. Or his fingers. Or—

All of it. It was *all* of it.

Because he played my body like he was born to do it, every touch and stroke winding me tighter, every brush of his tongue pushing me closer to the edge.

"Oh God, Damon," I groaned. "Like that. Please just . . . *oh God!*"

I exploded, a shower of sparks bursting behind my eyelids, pleasure surging through my limbs, my pussy clenching around his fingers as firmly as my hands clenched in his hair.

It seemed to go on forever, wave after wave of liquid heat coating my skin, flooding through my nerves, making my head spin.

The moment I regained the tiniest bit of use of my body, I was tugging at his head, pulling him up my body. "Now," I whispered. "Please."

His underwear disappeared, the condom was grabbed off the nightstand and rolled on, and he was back between my thighs, pushing in, filling me, stretching me . . . expanding me.

And not just my body.

But my heart was expanding right alongside it.

Then he moved, and I stopped thinking about feelings. Instead, I just *felt*.

Him pulling out and pressing in, his thumb drifting down to my clit, his lips on mine, tongue delving into my mouth, encouraging mine to tangle with his. It was . . . everything and also just the smallest sliver of a moment, our movements crystallized down to a single shared heartbeat, a sharp exhale, a burst of pleasure.

"Come on, baby," he panted, thumb working my clit, sweat on his forehead. "Come for me."

I wasn't far off, sprinting up and up, spinning higher, winding tighter until I fell over the edge with a cry.

He groaned. "That's it, baby."

One stroke. Two. Three.

And Damon joined me in plummeting over the other side.

The best part?

Him holding me close as our heartbeats began to slow, his fingers running through my hair, him whispering, "I love you."

Me whispering back, "I love you, too."

FIFTEEN

Damon

OKAY, so perhaps bringing Eden to my parents' house when we were still new, just beginning to figure out our future together wasn't the best idea.

My mom stood on the front porch, hair tugged into a ponytail, jeans and bright purple sweater encasing her—as she liked to call them—kiddy curves. My father always said she was beautiful, no matter that she complained about the extra weight gained during three pregnancies she'd never been able to fully shed.

It was true, not the weight or the change in size, but that my mom was beautiful.

She had a light inside her that only seemed to grow brighter through the years. Charisma or charm, or maybe it was simply that she seemed to care about everyone she met, no matter if they were the checkout clerk at the grocery store or her hairdresser.

"She's beautiful," Eden murmured, head turning so she could smile up at me.

My heart squeezed, and I knew she got it, knew she could see, even from a distance that the beauty of my mom came not from the outward appearance—though my mom *was* an attractive woman—but because of what was inside.

Cliché.

But sometimes clichés were true.

Eden understood that. She knew what it was like to be judged on her outside appearance, but she also knew what it was to deal with a monster lurking beneath the veneer of innocence. What was inside was critically important, cliché or not.

"Yes, she is," I agreed, maneuvering my car into my spot, or what had been my spot during high school. With three teenagers in the house and multiple sports and extra-curriculars and five cars between us, parking had been undertaken with military precision.

Though my car was a lot nicer now.

"What are you smiling about?" Eden asked as I turned off the engine.

"I was thinking about the old beater that somehow managed to get me from school and sports and back when I was in high school."

Her lips curved. "At least you had a car?"

"There is that, though my friends always teased it was more rust than metal." I popped my door and started to get out, pausing to glance back at her. "Didn't stop them from bumming a ride, though."

Her laughter trailed me around to the trunk of my car, but before I could open it, my mom was there, and I was wrapped in the quintessential Mom Hug. Warm, soft yet firm, and filled with her scent. Roses and vanilla, which I knew was her favorite because I always shipped her a big box of lotion, soap, and other womanly things every year for her birthday.

"You've been gone too long," she said.

Of course, she always said *that*, but this time she was right. I hadn't been home in months, and I hadn't quite realized how much I'd missed it until I was here, surrounded by redwoods, moisture in the air, the mountains in the distance.

Same state, different world.

"I'm glad I'm here now."

One more squeeze and she jumped back. "Oh dear, I'm being terribly rude in ignoring your friend."

"Hi," Eden said with a wave. She'd come out of the car and was standing a few feet away, smile on her lips. "I'm Eden. It's nice to meet you. Damon has told me so much about you. I hope you don't mind me crashing his visit."

My mom glanced at me, eyes wide and warm, before crossing over to Eden and pulling her into a hug. "Mind? Dear, it's so lovely to meet you. *Carrot* was one of my favorite films ever."

Eden blushed.

"Now, now," my mom tutted. "No blushing. You're a fabulous actress, and I can't wait to see what else you've made."

"Thank you, Mrs. Garcia."

"Anabelle, please." My mom wound her arm through Eden's. "Or Belle. Or hey you, I'm hungry and need food."

Eden glanced up at her. "I'm sorry?"

My mom chuckled. "Sorry, I always joke that was my name when my house was filled with teenagers. Here, now, come on into the house."

Eden hesitated, turned back to me. "I should get my bag."

"Pish. Damon's got them."

I blew her a kiss when her bright emerald eyes met mine. "I wouldn't dream of making a big movie star carry her own things."

Those pretty eyes narrowed.

My mom tutted. "He's just teasing you."

Eden laughed. "Oh, I know all about Damon and his teasing."

A beat, a shared grin. Then, my mom continued tugging her toward the house and I heard Eden say, "So was he also teasing when he said you'd share your world-famous French toast recipe with me?"

My mom mock-gasped. "How dare he promise I give away my spoils?" A beat. "But seriously, I'd be happy to share it. I can only cook a few things really well, but that's one of them—"

"She's lying!" I called, tugging our bags from the trunk. "Everything she cooks is delicious."

"I paid him to say that," my mom stage-whispered.

"Well, let's hope I can pay him to say the same," Eden said. "Because I can make one thing and that thing is blueberry pancakes."

"Well"—my mom patted Eden's arm—"I'll share my French toast if you share your pancakes."

"Hey!" I accused, coming up behind them. "I've begged you for that recipe for years!"

"You're not worthy," my mom tossed over her shoulder as they headed up the porch steps. "It's girls only."

"Ouch!" I mimed getting stabbed in the chest. "Five minutes and I'm already tossed to the side. Your only son, betrayed and left wanting."

Eden grinned. "There are those acting skills again." She glanced down at my mom. "I keep telling him that he should put them to use, Belle. In fact, there's this perfect role in a script I was just sent."

"Oh!" My mom dropped her arms, or rather put them up to her face. "I've said the same! He's so talented and—"

I dropped the bags and darted forward to scoop Eden up and toss her over my shoulder. "You're going to pay for that, baby." I clamped one hand over her legs to hold her in place and the other I brought up to her waist, tickling in the spot I'd discovered just the night before.

"Damon!" she shrieked, but she was laughing and squirming . . . and so was my mom—well, laughing, that was. She'd scooped up the bags and gone ahead of us, holding the door so I could carry Eden through.

"Quick! Into the closet, Damon," my mom said over the sound of Eden's protesting. "That's where we keep all of our captives."

I snorted so hard I almost lost my grip on Eden.

My fingers faltered, but Eden lost it.

My mom lost it.

And I followed suit.

I knew that this weekend was going to be absolutely perfect.

I just didn't realize it was going to decimate me when it was over.

SIXTEEN

Eden

I DID GET the French toast recipe and Damon was right, it *was* delicious. I also tried my hand at making tortillas and quickly discovered that they were well outside of my limited cooking skills.

Damon snagged the lopsided lump of dough I'd mangled away from me. "Um, nice job?"

I took it back with glarey eyes, trying to smooth it out with my hands. "Not all round foods are created equal."

Belle tutted, reshaped the mound in a perfectly round ball. "Try again, dear."

"Pancakes, I can do," I muttered, placing it in the tortilla maker, closing the top, and then pulling down firmly on the handle, exactly like she'd shown me.

Except, it wasn't *exactly*, was it?

Otherwise, when I opened the round plate, I would have revealed a perfect tortilla instead of . . . whatever it was that I'd just made.

Not even. Not smooth. Not . . . good.

"Ugh," I muttered.

"Why don't you crumble the cheese, Eden?"

Sighing, I nodded then moved over to the block of white cheese Belle indicated. "Is this the stupid-proof job?"

"No, of course not," Belle protested.

But Damon was nodding and smirking.

"So, I'm not good at shredding pork, I can't make tortillas, I burned the beans, and . . . now you dare put me in charge of the cheese?"

"Um . . ." Belle bit her lip. "Okay, it's pretty much stupid-proof." A beat. "Unless you drop the block on the floor."

"Like this?" I mimed dropping it.

Belle gasped then lightly smacked me on the arm. "Don't even pretend to joke about my cheese."

"It's her favorite," Damon stage-whispered. "Plus, you'll redeem yourself by making us guacamole later."

Belle lifted a brow.

"It might even be better than yours," Damon teased.

A gasp, but Belle was smiling.

"I can make guac later. I'm sure it wouldn't stand up against yours though," I said and began breaking off chunks of the cheese, mimicking what I'd seen in the multitude of Mexican restaurants I'd eaten at. Hopefully, I was doing at least that right.

But I supposed if I wasn't, it was still cheese, so there were worse problems in the world than the wrong sized cheese crumbles.

"You know," I said. "I just signed on to do a film where I'll be playing a chef."

Silence, Damon's and Belle's eyes shooting toward mine, wide in surprise.

Then Belle's lips twitched. Mine followed suit. Damon held

it together for another beat . . . but then we all burst into laughter.

"Now, that's a happy sound," a male voice said.

I turned, saw an older man who was the very picture of Damon, though a little softer around the jaw and waistline and with a little more gray in his hair.

Despite that, it was absolutely clear that he was Damon's father, Diego.

DNA, man, it was a bitch.

Whipping toward Damon, I jabbed my finger in his direction. "*That* is what you're going to look like as you get older?" I dropped the block of cheese to the plate and plunked my hands to my hips. "Why is it that men always get more handsome with age and woman just get . . . lumpy and wrinkled?"

Bella snorted.

Diego's lips curved. "I think she's saying I'm handsome."

Horror washed over me. Had I really just said that? In front of a man I didn't know? In front of Damon's father? I mean, I felt like I knew him, based on this afternoon and all the stories Damon and Belle had told me. "I'm sorry, that was incredibly rude."

His brows pulled down, face falling. "Are you saying I'm *not* handsome?"

"Oh, no." I wrung my hands together. "You're *absolutely* handsome. You—" His lips twitched, just barely, but I'd seen that same look on Damon's face enough to recognize mischief.

And so I put my acting skills to work.

I let tears well in my eyes then covered my mouth with my hand, choking back a sob and turning toward the plate, head hanging. "I'm sorry," I said weekly. "I'm so s-sorry—"

More silence in the kitchen, though this time it wasn't trailed by laughter.

A hand on my shoulder.

Not Damon's, but Belle's.

"It's okay—"

I glanced at her out of the corner of my eye, and she took one glance at my face before a wide smile broke out on her lips. Then she burst out laughing. "I'm sorry," she said between giggles. "I didn't mean— To ruin— Your joke—"

"Joke?" Diego asked.

Belle nodded. "It seems that Eden fits right in with us and our pranks."

Damon tugged me away from the counter and into his arms. "That's because Eden is perfect"—he dropped his voice—"and perfect for me."

I scoffed. "Hardly."

He rested his chin on my shoulder. "Perfect."

"She'll be perfect if she can finish crumbling that cheese," Belle said, patting my arm. "And you'll"—she tugged Damon back to the tortilla maker—"be perfect if you get going on the dough."

"And I'll be perfect"—Diego reached for one of the forks that was in the shredded pork Belle had rescued from my incompetent hands—"at eating this delicious—*ow!*"

Belle had smacked the fork out of Diego's hand.

"You'll be perfect at washing up and then getting the table set."

The disappointment on Diego's face would have fit right in with the rom-com I'd just finished filming, but Belle had no sympathy. She shooed him off. "Nice try. But I'm guessing by the smell of oil and sawdust on your clothes, you've been out with the crew all day."

"They were building a new robot today."

"Oh! What kind of robot?" I'd heard about how Diego had worked his way up from a tech to a senior engineer at the company he was working at. Something about artificial intelligence and drones and food deliveries. Apparently, they were contracted to build them for some big company based out of San Francisco.

Diego grinned, coming over to wash his hands at the sink next to me. "A flying robot."

"That's so cool!" I exclaimed.

"Well, I think it's pretty cool I got to meet you," Diego said. "Damon doesn't exactly bring a lot of girls home. Especially famous ones."

"I'm not *so* famous," I said.

"She's lying," Damon interjected. "Or at least minimizing. Paparazzi are all over her in L.A." A beat. "But lucky for me, that meant I got to keep her mostly to myself instead of going out."

"It just meant you were able to bribe me with delicious carbs in order to spin your web of love around me."

"Love?" he asked, extracting a perfect tortilla from the press. His mom barely let him lift the plate before she'd snagged it and placed it in the pan on the stove to start cooking it. "Or lies?"

"Either." I grinned, finished with the cheese and moved to the sink to wash. "Both."

Damon snagged my waist as I moved across the kitchen, intending to help his dad set the table. "Relax, love."

I spun in the circle of his arms, hand coming up to rub the pleasant ache in my chest, not just from him showing me unbridled affection in front of his family, but also because . . . of his family. They were wonderful.

"This . . . I *am* relaxed, baby. I—I've never been in a place like this, been so comfortable or welcomed. It's like"—my voice dropped to a whisper—"I'm part of it. Like because they made you, you wonderful man, that they know exactly how to get under my armor and—"

I broke off, blinking back real tears this time.

"I understand," he whispered. "You know I do."

"Thanks for letting me come."

He grinned. "Thanks for not dumping me when I was an ass."

"Thanks for loving me."

"Thanks for loving me back."

His lips came down onto mine and he kissed me. I forgot about his parents and the hot stove, I forgot about the evil tortilla maker and the shredded pork and the crumbled cheese. I got lost in the feel of Damon, in the taste of his mouth, in his spicy smell, in the way his body felt pressed to mine.

I forgot about everything.

Except what was most important.

Damon.

But because I'd forgotten about everything, I didn't realize my cell wasn't in my pocket, that it was in his car when my agent tried to reach me.

Then Maggie.

Neither Damon nor I knew that my world was imploding around me.

SEVENTEEN

Damon

MY CELL RANG from its place on the nightstand.

Groaning and feeling like I'd just fallen asleep, I saw it was just after three in the morning.

And my sister Colleen was calling.

Even though she lived on the East Coast, it was only six there, and my sister was *not* a morning person.

"Hello?" I answered, heart in my throat.

"Damon," she said quickly. "Mom—uh—mentioned you were dating Eden Larsen. Is that right?"

Okay, not the conversational starting point I'd expected. I sat up, slipping out of bed and into the hall so as to not wake Eden. What, did she want premiere tickets or perhaps a hookup on some new fashion trend? Colleen *did* have an obsession with fancy heels. "We're dating," I confirmed cautiously.

"Right." Her voice was troubled. "Well, I just . . . I guess I wanted to see if she was okay."

My heart had been in my throat. Now it dropped somewhere in the direction of the floor. "What are you saying, Collie?"

"Just . . . with the stories in the news and—"

Forget the floor.

My heart was sinking into the fucking foundation.

"What stories?"

"The ones about her . . . um . . . child marriage."

"Please, tell me this is one of your jokes."

Silence.

"Collie." Yes, I was begging.

And my sister knew it. "Damon, you know I wouldn't use something like this as a joke. It's . . . they're everywhere."

"Oh God," I said. "Fuck. Where's *everywhere*? What networks are the stories on?"

"All the morning shows," she said. "But I saw it on Facebook when I woke up this morning. It's . . . I know I shouldn't be on my phone first thing, but I was and it's there and . . . in the *Times*, too, Damon." Her voice was gentle. "It's the front-page story everywhere."

I'd dropped to my knees, not having realized it until Eden was in front of me, crouching down, eyes wide and face concerned. "What's the matter?"

"I have to go, Collie," I said into the phone.

"Okay," she whispered. "Tell her I'm so sorry this is happening."

"I will," I forced out between numb lips and hung up.

"Damon?" Eden placed her palm on my cheek. "What's the matter?"

She was comforting me. Eden's life had imploded, and she was comforting me. Of course, she didn't *know* her life had imploded because—

Fuck.

I jumped up, took her hand. "Come back into my room," I said. "We need to get your publicist on the phone, first thing."

"Damon?" she asked again, concern clouding her eyes.

"Now, baby." Shit. How could I tell her this? "There are some news stories."

Eden laughed, that concern disappearing. "News stories? Is that all? Baby, there are always stories online and on the gossip shows about me. Trust me, this isn't something to be concerned about."

I kept tugging her hand until she was back in the bedroom, sitting on the edge of the queen-sized bed my parents had put in after they'd relegated my sports trophies and swimsuit posters to boxes in the garage. Only when she was sitting did I crouch in front of her, my hands on her knees. "Sweetheart," I said. "I need your phone."

"You're scaring me."

"I know. I'm sorry, but Eden, we need to call your publicist. Right now."

She nodded, cheeks gone pale, moisture clouding the green of her eyes. "It should be in my purse?" She snagged it, emptying the contents onto the bed. But no phone. "Or maybe my bag?"

But when I'd emptied that, it wasn't there either.

"When did you last have it?"

"Damon, you need to tell me what's going on."

"Phone first, baby," I said. "Then—" I shook my head. "Did you have it at dinner?"

Her brows drew together. "No, I didn't. I don't think I had it all afternoon." She stared at her hands for a few seconds. "I don't think I've used it since the car ride."

I nodded, jumped to my feet and grabbed my keys. "I'll go get it."

"Okay."

Taking the stairs two at a time, I ran down the hall and out the front door. Less than two minutes later, I'd found it in the cup holder and brought it straight back upstairs.

But I'd been too slow.

I heard the voice of the news reporter as I hit the top of the stairs . . .

"Shocking news today as early reports of Eden Larsen's child marriage appears to be true. According to state records, she was wed at thirteen to a Tim Williams, who was twenty-seven years her senior. The controversy of this has been unparalleled, especially as Ms. Larsen has not yet issued a statement. I have an expert on the state-by-state laws of under-aged marriage on the line, let's go to her now . . ."

"Shit," I said, bursting into the room.

Eden was already on her feet, yanking a sweatshirt from her bag and slipping it over her head.

"Baby—"

"I trusted you," she said, pain turning her features severe. "I confided in you, and you told someone."

"I didn't—"

Her hands worked in rapid succession, shoving items back into her purse, her feet into her shoes, and all the while the TV blared on in the background.

"I—"

"No." The word was sharper than I'd ever heard from her and edged with the same panic as the scene in her bedroom all those weeks before.

"Honey, I didn't tell anyone. I would never—"

She swept a hand toward the TV. *"Then how do they know?"* she screamed.

I heard a thump from down the hall, the sounds of footsteps coming toward us, along with concerned voices. My parents appeared behind me in the doorframe. "Is everything—?"

The sob that emerged from Eden's throat was like that of a wounded animal.

And it wounded me.

She grabbed her purse, left her bag, and then ran by me.

"Damon?" my mom asked.

"It's—" I shook my head, not able to reassure my mom that it was going to be okay, not when the thing that pained Eden the most was out in the world for all to see and gawk at and comment on. Not when it would spurn the next cycle of news, be exploited for days and days on end by experts and—

"Honey." My mom put her hand on my arm. "What can I do?"

My throat burned. "Nothing, Mom," I said. "No one can do anything."

I hustled back down the stairs, through the front door, across the yard to the car.

Where Eden was standing, her hands on the roof of it, her purse at her feet.

My feet crunched across the gravel.

She spun, her despair evident even in the moonlight.

"I'll drive you wherever you need to go, baby. But I'm not leaving you."

Her face crumpled.

Her legs collapsed.

And her knees hit the gravel hard before I had a chance to move.

Some hero.

I couldn't even protect the woman I loved from skinned knees.

But then I was there next to her, tentatively reaching for her hand, scared she was going to push me away, terrified we'd be right back in that panic from her bedroom.

Instead, the moment I touched her, she spun and crawled

into my lap, knocking me to my ass. She burrowed against my chest, sobs puffing against my throat and tears soaking through the fabric of my shirt. The gravel hurt, but not as much as the agony of Eden's tears as I held her tight.

I don't know how long she cried or how long I sat there holding her as she wept, but eventually I heard the soft footsteps of someone approaching.

My mom was there, a blanket in hand. She wrapped it around Eden as gently as one would swaddle a newborn . . . and I knew she'd seen the story blaring on the TV in my room.

She touched my shoulder, scooped up Eden's purse, and then disappeared into the house.

"I'm sorry, Damon," Eden whispered, slipping her arms around my waist, eyes wet when she glanced up at me. "I shouldn't have said that. I know you didn't tell anyone."

I wiped my thumbs across her cheeks, trying to dry her tears, but they kept coming, continued dripping out of the corners of her eyes. "It's okay, love."

"It's not."

"Shh, now. We'll figure it out later."

"Together?" More tears. "You won't leave?"

"No, baby. I'm here."

She nodded, burrowing back against my chest. "I'm so sorry."

"Shh," I murmured. "It's going to be okay." We didn't talk further or call her publicist. We didn't do anything but sit there, with our arms around each other as the moon moved across the sky and the sun began to rise.

EIGHTEEN

Eden

"COME ON, NOW," Belle said. "Just a couple of bites of toast."

Obliging her, I picked up the toast and brought it to my lips, but I might as well have been trying to eat cardboard.

I chewed and chewed and *chewed*, but couldn't swallow it down.

Gagging, I spit it into a napkin.

"It's okay, baby," she murmured. "Forget about the toast." Her hand rubbed the space between my shoulder blades lightly. A motherly touch, one I didn't even realize I hadn't *ever* had.

The church had been my family.

Then I'd lost it.

I'd lost everything and retreated and closed down and . . .

Now I was sitting in Belle's kitchen surrounded by people who cared for me, one who'd been patient for years, two who'd accepted me because I made their son happy. I shook my head firmly, trying to dislodge the fog out that had settled in my brain when I'd heard the story.

This kitchen. This place. These people.

They could be my family.

No, they *were* my family.

If I let them.

That, more than anything else, snapped me out of my head. I could come back to this kitchen, I could learn how to make decent tortillas, I could perfect that French toast recipe, and figure out how to properly shred pork . . . if I let them in.

My cell was on the table in front of me, turned to silent because of the sheer volume of calls and texts. Including several dozen from Maggie.

Who I needed to call first thing.

But I kept seeing the reporter's face from that show, the near-smirk as he'd reported on what was probably the biggest story of his life, triumph and pleasure all wrapped up with my past.

There would be more like that. More triumph, more crowing, more analyzing every titillating face.

Breaking down what had gone wrong, what *I'd* done wrong.

And it would be horrible.

My eyes welled with tears again, but I blinked them back. I couldn't keep sitting here, crying and sobbing over toast, not doing anything, keeping people who were trying to show they cared about me at a distance.

Because if I did that, I discounted everything else, including the fact that I'd survived.

I'd been a young and impressionable girl and . . . I'd been hurt by the people who should have looked out for me.

That was the story.

And I needed to get it out there.

"Can you hand me my phone?" I asked Damon. He and Diego were sitting across from me, concern on their faces.

"Sweetheart?"

I'd earned that concern, but I was going to ease it.

"I'll be okay now." I put out my hand.

"You need more time—"

"I'm going to be okay, baby," I said. "I can do this. With you, all of you, I can figure this out."

Diego's face was soft, and he patted Damon on the shoulder. "Hand her the phone, son."

Damon shook his head. "I should protect her."

My heart pulsed with pain, with hope, with *love*, and any remaining armor I'd been clinging to disappeared.

It clanged against that tile floor and for the first time in more than a decade, I felt as though I were able to take a deep breath. Without pain, without straining, with nothing but a simple inhale and exhale.

I could do this.

I *had* to do this.

Because I wanted my happy future, and I wanted it with Damon.

And his family.

He handed me the cell. I called Maggie, then my agent, then the studio, and the next few days were a blurred flurry of events.

Only when everything calmed and the dust had settled, I couldn't believe who was at the center of it.

THE CAMERAS FOUND us on the second day, descending on Diego and Belle's driveway like black-lensed locusts, reporters knocking on the door, shouting my name.

Diego had called off work, Belle was holed up in the kitchen cooking, and I was trying to figure out what to do. Or rather my team was, since the story only seemed to grow larger.

The media had gone to my hometown and found out about the pregnancy, since it was still apparently local gossip.

The judge's name who'd signed off on the marriage had been released along with photos of a young me from the hospital, arm casted, bruises blooming on my side, a fat lip.

That had been after I'd lost the baby.

But before I'd lost Tim . . . or been freed from him anyway. Which was probably not a charitable thing to be thinking about someone who passed away, but I didn't have enough *charity* in me to wish him anything but the end he'd met.

My phone rang. I set down the tortilla dough I was rolling—because at least I'd gotten better at the first part of the exercise—and glanced down at the screen. It was a number I didn't recognize, and I'd learned enough over the last forty-eight hours to immediately reject any caller I didn't know.

It began ringing again. Just like it had for that entire morning. Just like it had since my number had somehow gotten out the previous evening.

Damon noticed, snagging it from the counter next to me and powering it off.

"I—"

He shook his head, shoved it in his pocket.

"Maggie might need to get ahold of me."

"She has my number, remember?"

"Yeah." I nodded, going to work on the next ball, hating that Damon was involved.

He pushed the dough away, leaned back against the counter next to me. "What's this?"

I shook my head. "Nothing. It's—"

Chocolate eyes met mine, held mine in place when I wanted to look away.

But I wasn't going to look away.

"Baby."

I sighed. "I'm struggling," I murmured. "This would be so much easier for you, for your family, if we just weren't together."

His hand dropped to my arm. "Don't say that."

I spun away. "How can I not?" I reached for the dough again but stopped when Damon shifted to the side, blocking me. I threw up my hands. "Your dad couldn't go to work this morning. Your mom had to unplug the phone. They can't go in their front yard. Because of me!"

"This isn't your fault."

"I know!" I snapped, pacing away. "And I love you for saying that, for being so calm and patient when you wouldn't have even been involved in this if it weren't for me, but—"

He stepped in front of me mid-pace, snagging my shoulders, and halting my progress. "I'm here because I love you."

I sniffed. "But your parents, this was just supposed to be a quick, fun visit, and I've ruined it." Another sniff. "They're prisoners in their own house!"

"They're fine," Damon said. "Maggie promised your phone with the new number would be here today. You two will get an uninterrupted conversation and can figure out your next step—"

"That's just it," I said. "I don't *know* my next step. The studio has delayed filming for a few weeks, offered another PR firm to help, but I *don't know what to do.*"

"You'll figure it out."

"What Damon?" I asked, pulling out of his hold. "My next move is *what?* Should I become some sort of ambassador for marriage laws? I want them to be changed, absolutely," I said. "No one should be married off at thirteen or fourteen or at any age before they can rationally consent. But my marriage wasn't the worst of it. There were so many issues intertwined that made it complicated." I went over to the tortilla-maker, shoving a ball of dough inside, and pulling down harshly on the handle. I yanked it back open to reveal a perfect tortilla inside.

So, that was the key to smoothly round circles of dough.

A proper dose of rage about the past.

"What makes it complicated?"

I grabbed another ball, put it inside. "I was preyed upon by a predator, not protected by my parents," I said and closed it. "I was failed by a legal system that allowed for one judge to sign off on a *thirteen*-year-old getting married." Open . . . to reveal another perfect tortilla.

Great. I was on a roll. Finally.

"And," I said, powering my way through more dough. "My experience wasn't a one-off. *Two hundred thousand* minors are married a year. *Just in the US.*" Another tortilla, another ball of dough. "Not all of those were thirteen or fourteen or even all female, of course, but *too* many were too young, too naïve, and forced, coaxed, or threatened into marriage." I sniffed, blinking back tears. "And those numbers don't begin to speak about the twelve million girls around the world who marry before they're eighteen. Many are preyed upon like I was. They miss out on school, aren't safe and protected, don't have access to birth control, have high-risk pregnancies because they can't seek good health care, and there isn't anyone who is looking after them—"

Soft, warm hands covered mine on the tortilla maker's handle. Not Damon's this time, but Bella's.

"And *there's* your next step, darling," she said.

I turned to face Bella. "What?"

She tsked, thumb coming up to wipe beneath each eye. "These girls need you," she murmured. "You have a chance to help some of them."

"But—" I shook my head. "I don't know where to begin. I'm not . . . an expert on social progress. I don't make policy. I'm just a girl who happened to live through a common experience."

"*That's* why," Damon whispered. "Because you understand.

You don't need to create a policy or to drive forward social progress. You just need to share your past."

"But so many have gone through so much worse."

"No." Belle cupped my cheeks for a moment before letting go. "You don't get to do that. You don't get to minimize the trauma you went through because you think someone else had it worse. Your trauma doesn't have to be quantified to be real."

"I—"

My words faltered. I didn't know what to say to that. She was right, of course, I wouldn't dare tell another person to not be hurt just because someone else might have been hurt *more*.

"I know your parents failed you," Belle murmured, "and I'm so sorry for that. I also know I'm meddling in your life when we've just begun to know each other and that you have every right to tell me to go to Hell—"

"Belle, I wouldn't—"

"I know," she murmured. "Because I see the way you look at my son. I saw the way you looked through his camera lens, your pain piercing my heart when Damon showed me that photograph all those years ago. I see the shadows in your eyes and the way you lift your chin to keep moving forward. You're a good person, Eden."

Damon slipped his arm around my shoulders just when my lips parted, readying to argue or protest or . . . I don't know, do something to discount how much those words meant. "I love you," he murmured. "And *this* is how real parents act. They support, they love without restriction." A kiss to my temple. "Because you're worthy of love, baby. *So* worthy."

"Yes," Belle said softly "You are, sweetie. Without qualification."

"I don't—" I broke off, eyes drifting away, so many emotions knotting in my stomach, so much of my past wanting to jump forward and deny the words. But then I saw that Diego was leaning against the doorframe, eyes soft, but expression gentle.

"She's right," he murmured.

I sucked in a long, slow breath. Released it.

But then my lips curved, tucked what they were telling me safely inside my heart and said, "Words a woman loves to hear."

Diego nodded at Damon. "Take notes, son."

Damon chuckled. "I am. Believe me, I am."

Diego came over to us, gently squeezing my arm. "You're welcome here, welcome to stay as long as you need. Honestly, working from home is a treat—"

"You say that now."

"No," Belle said. "He says it because his team is thrilled to not have him underfoot, and he can have a beer at three in the afternoon."

Diego didn't refute this, just headed to the fridge and extracted a bottle. I glanced at the clock, and the rest of my melancholy faded . . . because it was three minutes after three in the afternoon.

"Clockwork," Belle murmured.

I grinned then felt my eyes burn again. They were just so wonderful and different from what I'd grown up with. It was almost like being in a dream or a movie scene. I was going to wake up or the director would call cut, and I'd be right back to where I was before.

And all of this wonderful would be gone.

Damon tugged me a little closer and I rested my head on his shoulder. "I guess, I never dreamed that your family might be like this."

"Meddling?" Belle asked lightly, nudging us aside and going to work on the tortillas. At this rate, we'd be making enough to start our own line of them.

"Lovely," I said, nuzzling into his chest. "Accepting." I

inhaled. "I should have known because Damon is so special, but I never even began to hope that I might be able to be part of something so wonderful."

Belle continued to crank through the dough. "Part of why I care, sweetie, is because your love for my son is so bright in your eyes." Her eyes drifted to mine. "And the other is because you're absolutely wonderful and deserve it."

Words. Just words.

But they wove their way into my heart as effectively as Damon had, as effectively as his parents had, and instead of tying me up, instead of dragging me down to Earth by the ankles, they lifted me up. They gave me courage and the wings to soar.

I could do this.

I could make a difference.

"I have a chance here," I whispered, more to myself than the room at large. "And I'm not going to waste it."

NINETEEN

Damon

EDEN WAS IN MY PARENTS' living room, a camera opposite her, Maggie, her publicist, hovering nearby, and she was
speaking to the primetime anchorwoman, when the news hit.

I noticed Maggie first, or rather the cell phone that kept
vibrating in her hand, her eyes repeatedly flicking down at it,
her face growing increasingly pale.

Then I saw the producer of the segment do the same, her
eyes growing wide.

And finally, *my* cell began to buzz.

Colleen.

That fucking asshole.

Along with that sentiment, she'd sent a link to a story with
the headline, *Emails Leaked Show that Grant Seagurio Hired PI
to Expose Eden Larsen's Past.*

"What the fuck?" I exclaimed, interrupting Eden's
announcement that she'd just partnered with several organiza-

tions and was starting her own to look into the problem of child marriage here and abroad.

At least my interruption hadn't been while she was discussing her past.

Still, it was jarring enough that both Eden and the news anchor's heads whipped in my direction. Eden took one glance at my face and pushed out of the chair, coming toward me.

"What's the matter?" she asked.

I showed her my phone. She clicked on the link and began reading what was inside.

"It was revealed today that Grant Seagurio, the star of Somewhere, From the Top, *and the horror franchise,* Hammer Head, *apparently hired the private investigator that discovered the marriage from Eden Larsen's past. The following emails were released by the private investigator, Hank Talbot, after Mr. Seagurio refused to pay Mr. Talbot's fees. They detail the actor's need to find a way to discredit Ms. Larsen because he was upset that she'd received top billing and a larger trailer for their joint project . . ."*

THE ARTICLE WENT on to detail that Talbot had, at first, refused to send over what he'd discovered but that Grant had promised to pay double. Money had talked, the files were shared, and Eden's past was splashed over the world.

And Talbot hadn't gotten his money anyway.

"What the fuck?" Eden whispered. "Grant?"

Maggie came over, her cell glued to her ear. "The emails look legitimate," she said, and then it seemed like someone on the other end of her phone call began speaking because she took off for the hall, voice carrying. "We need absolutely everyone on this . . ."

"Damon?" Eden shook her head and I wrapped my arms around her, in just as much shock. "*Grant?*" she repeated.

"I know," I said, holding her tightly. "I—"

Words failed me.

Grant?

"For a bigger trailer? Because my name was going to come first?"

I had nothing. Absolutely nothing. "People are assholes," I said, knowing it couldn't begin to encompass everything but also . . . it was the only thing I could think of to say.

Eden froze in my arms for a heartbeat then her head tilted back, and her green eyes met mine. Her mouth curved, her chest began rocking, and laughter emerged from between her lips.

It was so unexpected that I found myself locked into place.

God, she was so beautiful. Absolutely lovely and filled with hope and not sadness or anger like I'd expected.

Like *I* was.

"I'm okay," she murmured. "This can't hurt me anymore." She cupped my jaw, thumb lightly stroking. "I swear, love. I swear, I'm okay. This isn't a setback. This is . . . the world seeing how much an asshole Grant truly is." A beat. "Though maybe I should thank him. Now I don't have anything to hide, and I can help people."

My mom walked into the room, her eyes wide as she strode to the TV and turned it on.

There was Grant, standing on a street corner in what looked like New York, men in hoodies and carrying huge cameras swarming him, shouting questions. We watched as he shoved one paparazzo hard, they tussled, and then both went toppling.

"And there goes an assault charge," Maggie said, having

popped her head back in. I stared at her agape, wondering how she could joke, how *Eden* could at a time like this, but then I realized I would probably never fully understand the workings of the female mind. Clearly, Maggie and Eden were a good fit together and that was all that mattered.

Well, that and also that this turn in Eden's story hadn't torn her to shreds.

She didn't need her armor.

She just needed me . . . to resist confronting Grant in person and showing him how hard *I* could shove.

I wanted to kill the bastard.

But I'd refrain.

For Eden. Because she'd turned this hell into something positive, and she didn't need me transforming it into some sort of sideshow by protecting her in all the wrong ways.

I'd take care of her in my own way.

And it would begin with pizza.

Because it was Thursday, and we weren't going to break with tradition.

Not when we finally had nothing but our future to look forward to.

Tonight, however, instead of ordering for two, I ordered for ten. The news anchor and her crew were just about to shoot the biggest story of their careers thus far.

They deserved to be full of carbs and cheese while they did so.

TWENTY

Eden

I HUGGED BELLE TIGHTLY. "Thank you. For everything."

She pulled back slightly. "Are you sure you can't stay for a while longer?"

"No," I told her. "You guys need to get back to normal."

"What about you, Eden? How are you going to get back to normal?"

"This *is* my new normal," I said. "I'll be okay."

"*We'll* be okay." Damon slipped an arm around my waist, tucked me close, and took the bag from my hand. "You've done the hard part," he murmured. "The rest we'll figure out together."

"Yes, we will."

I sucked in a breath, released it slowly. "Okay, let's do this."

Belle opened the front door. "Holler if you need me to come out and tell them what's what." Her eyes narrowed. "Parasites," she muttered. "All of them."

The paparazzi that had hung around certainly were persistent. And maybe parasitic in some way, because though there was a place for them in my industry, I was hard-pressed to justify their presence in Belle and Diego's front yard for days on end, trampling their plants, kicking up their gravel.

"You'll be free of them soon," I assured her. "And most of them will trail us as soon as we leave, so you and Diego can get back to normal."

"Oh, that's not what I meant at all," she exclaimed. "I—"

I squeezed her hand. "I know."

Then one more breath, one more glance around a house that was smaller than mine in L.A., one that was worn and lived-in and not luxurious, but one that was more comfortable, more of a real home than any I'd ever resided in.

A sniff. "Come back soon," she said, and it was more order than request.

"I will," I reassured her, not minding the order in the least.

I'd spent just one week with these people, and through it, endured one of the most miserable times of my life, and yet . . . this period had also been filled with some of the best of days of my twenty-eight years.

And now to face the gauntlet, to move on and forward . . . and to make a difference instead of hiding beneath my armor.

"Thank you," I said again. "For . . . being more of a mother to me in a week than I've ever had."

Belle sniffed.

I sniffed.

Damon tugged me against his chest.

Diego tugged Belle against his.

We all stood there for a moment, quiet and thoughtful. They should have been strangers and yet . . . they weren't. Because of Damon, because of how they'd welcomed me into their little family with open arms.

Finally, Belle pulled away and sighed. "You're coming back

for Thanksgiving *and* Christmas." Another order. "Colleen and Cindy are dying to meet you."

I didn't mind *this* order either. Especially because this one made my lips twitch. I'd spoken to Colleen briefly on the phone, thanking her after Damon had mentioned she'd called trying to warn him when the story first broke. She was as sweet and kind and funny as the rest of the Garcia crew. "I'll be here," I said then poked Damon lightly. "We'll see about this one and his workaholic tendencies."

"Hey! I've got months off," he said in mock-outrage. "Meanwhile, the woman I love is spending the next three in Hawaii."

I reached for the doorknob, started to turn it. "You know the good thing about having all that time off?"

"What?"

"That you can spend it in Hawaii." I smiled as his eyes warmed then opened the door and stepped out. "With me."

That shot—me striding through the front door of Damon's parents' house, clad in jeans, sneakers, and a simple hoodie, hair in a red sheet behind me, my makeup simple, huge smile on my face as the man I loved looked out at me lovingly—made the front page of almost every paper in the world.

It had even more shares than the silver bikini.

SHOOTING ON *BORN FREE*, the action film set in Hawaii, was going much better than the rom-com with Grant, and it had been all of one day.

Or maybe that was because my male co-star wasn't an ass.

The surf and sun and beautiful sandy beaches didn't hurt much either.

I'd let the interview from the primetime show stand on its own for now, wanting to focus on finalizing plans for my charity and pulling together the staff who would run it. I could be the face and give the starting funds, but I didn't know how to best get help to those who need it, wasn't familiar with all of the laws and legalities of providing that assistance.

I just knew I wanted to help make a difference.

"Hey," Damon said, coming up behind me. He held a cup of coffee over my shoulder and I took it as he wrapped his arms around me.

"Thanks."

He rested his chin on my shoulder, both of us staring out the window . . . or maybe that was just me because a few moments later, he pressed his lips to my throat and murmured, "You're the most beautiful woman I've ever seen."

I snorted. "You've been around beautiful women your whole career." I took a sip from the mug then set it on the small table and spun to face him, my lips tilting up. "Not that I'm saying I won't take the compliment."

He slipped his hand into my hair. "Is that all it takes to get into your heart, sweetheart? Some pretty words?" His lips brushed mine.

"I'm easy," I teased.

"Not that," he murmured against my mouth. "But nothing worth it is ever easy."

"Mmm," I said and took his hand, leading him back toward the bed. "Well, come and show me how easy *you* are."

"What about the coffee?" he asked. "I fought with the coffeemaker for thirty minutes just to make that one cup."

I slipped the T-shirt I'd been wearing over my head, dropped it to the floor.

"What was that about coffee?"

He scooped me up into his arms and tossed me onto the bed. "Forget coffee." A brushing kiss to my lips, a nip to my throat. "How long until you have to be on set?" he asked.

"Hours yet."

He grinned then began kissing his way down my chest, my stomach, taking a moment to divert to my breasts.

I moaned, my fingers weaving into his hair, holding him to me.

"I think I can work with hours," he said against my skin.

A nip, a kiss, a flick of his tongue . . . and I knew he could, too.

I also knew he could work with days, with months.

With years.

And that I finally could, too.

EPILOGUE

Damon, Thanksgiving

"I CAN'T WAIT UNTIL CHRISTMAS," Colleen exclaimed. "Damon can be little orphan Annie again and—"

"Not on your life," I muttered.

Eden turned from where she was peeling potatoes over the sink. "I don't know, I'd love to see you in that curly red wig. Or better yet, with a perm."

I narrowed my eyes at her, but she just winked at Colleen and turned back to the potatoes. I'd known they would get on thick as thieves, but I hadn't expected the natural consequences of that.

Namely, that they'd turned their collective attention toward teasing me.

I protested and pretended to hate it, but in reality, I was thrilled that Eden had fit so perfectly into my family. She spoke to my mom almost more often than I did, had called Colleen several times before we'd met up for Thanksgiving. Cindy hadn't been able to get time off from work, but we would all be together at Christmas.

But besides the communicating, she'd jumped right in when we'd arrived two days before, teasing and joking, cooking—more than just blueberry pancakes—and sharing set secrets with Colleen and my mom.

In many ways, she was unrecognizable from the woman I'd known over the years.

And yet, she was the same.

Just . . . freer.

I nipped her ear and reached past her to grab the now naked potatoes, bringing them to my cutting board and cutting them into smaller chunks as my mom had ordered. Then into the pot they went. The turkey was done and cooling on the counter, the stuffing crisping in the oven, corn and bean salad on the table, along with rolls, and a side of tortillas Eden had insisted on making because she'd perfected the process.

She brought me the last potato when she finished it, which I cut and put into the pot.

Now finished with our assigned jobs, I snagged her hand and tugged her out into the backyard. My mom, elbow deep in pie crust, gave me a knowing look as we went.

Knowing because she knew what was in my pocket.

What was burning a *hole* in my pocket.

"Everything okay?" Eden asked.

I tucked my arm around her and guided us over to the steps, sitting down and tugging her into my lap. "I'm good. Just wanted a moment alone with you."

"A moment away from your family and the risk of you wearing that red, curly wig?"

"It doesn't go with my complexion," I deadpanned.

She laughed, rested her head on my shoulder, but didn't press me further.

We'd had a lot of moments like this over the last months, quiet and still, enjoying each other. Though, they were usually bookended by cameras—on set and on the street—and yelling—by fans or directors or paparazzi—but eventually, we always found our way back to quiet.

"Here," I said, reaching into my pocket and dropping the contents into Eden's palm.

Her eyes widened, mouth dropping open in surprise when she saw the dough I dropped into her hand.

Reasonably so, since it was out of left field.

"Um." She squeezed it lightly. "Is there a reason you've given me raw tortilla dough?"

I kissed her neck. "Not tortilla dough."

She spun to face me. "What?"

"It's *pizza* dough."

Her brows pulled down. "Still not making sense, baby."   .

"It's Thursday," I said.

"Yes, Thanksgiving typically does fall on a Thursday."

Those brows came up.

"It might be Thanksgiving, but it's still Pizza Night."

I saw the moment it clicked on her face, green eyes warming, her shoulders shaking, arms wrapping around me, lips pressing to mine. I kissed her for long minutes, but when we broke apart for air, I took her hand with the dough in mine and brought it between us.

"You're supposed to look inside."

"Look inside the ball of dough?"

I nodded.

One red brow lifted. "Are balls of dough *known* for containing surprises?"

"This one is."

She glanced from me to the dough then back again.

Sighing, I took it from her and tore it open . . . to reveal the ring inside.

Her breath caught. "Damon?"

"I love you, Eden," I said. "And I want to marry you, but if this is too much too soon, we'll shove it back into the ball of dough and keep it for another Pizza Night, one far into the future, one when you're ready."

"You'd put it back?" she asked, eyes serious.

I nodded, gut clenching. With everything going so well, I hadn't thought this would be too soon . . . but we hadn't even been dating a year and had been apart some of that. Not to mention her past.

"Yes," I said, stomach clenching. "I would."

"Because"—a shuddering breath—"this is a lot and—"

Mischief.

Creeping across green eyes.

I would have missed it if I didn't know her so well.

"Eden."

She giggled.

"I think I'd better put it back." I reached for the dough, started to fold it back around the diamond ring.

She gasped. "Don't you dare!"

I stood, dumping her onto the step next to me. "Nope. You don't want it and—"

Eden lurched off the deck and into my arms. "Stop, Damon. Don't get any more dough stuck in that gorgeous diamond setting. I *want* it. I want the ring and the Pizza Nights and I want *you*."

My heart leaped.

Her fingers brushed my jaw. "I love you so much and want *everything* I never dreamed I'd have."

I tossed the dough aside and slipped the ring on her finger. "I want *everything* with you, too," I told her. "I want our Pizza Nights and to keep finding ways to slip you away from set to sneak in a kiss. I want FaceTime and in person time and to hold your purse while you stand in front of the cameras capturing you in a beautiful dress at your premieres. But most of all, I just want you in my arms, as much as possible, for as long as possible."

She smiled. "I want that, too, Damon." A beat as her lips lowered to mine. "But sometimes I might wear pants."

"Well, I've already established that your ass looks amazing in pants, so I can deal with that."

She smacked me lightly.

I cupped her cheeks.

Then I kissed her.

And kept on kissing until Colleen threatened me through the kitchen door with that curly red wig again.

Eden giggled as she broke away, tugging me toward the house.

"Can't have that," she said as we went. "That's special for Christmas!"

Green eyes warm with laughter, with happiness and hope. Armor hung up on pegs.

The past. The present. A new family. A bright future.

Eden finally had it all.

And she'd given it all to me.

EPILOGUE

PART TWO

Maggie

MY CELL VIBRATED JUST as the minister declared, "You may kiss the bride."

Slipping out of my chair as Eden and Damon locked lips, but before they vacated the altar, I sprinted down the aisle and toward a tree, hustling behind it.

Only five people were currently on Do Not Disturb.

Eden—who was otherwise occupied.

Three additional equally important clients. All of who were either in attendance—and Pierce and Artie were not likely to be on the phone as they watched the bride and groom get hitched—or on the opposite side of the globe—and Talbot was probably sleeping.

The last was my father.

Who *never* called unless something was on fire, someone was bleeding out, or an asteroid was heading toward the planet.

I glanced at the screen, not realizing how much I'd been hoping it was Talbot with some earth-shattering crisis until I saw "Dad calling" flashing across the surface. "Shit," I muttered, swiping a finger and bringing it up to my ear. "Hi, Dad. Everything okay?"

"It's not Dad."

Hot then cold. Goose bumps on my arms. The past shoving its way firmly into my present, because his voice was ice and it broke my heart.

Aaron.

My *ex* Aaron.

My ex because *I'd* left.

"What's wrong?"

"Your father fell," Aaron said. "He's in the hospital."

"What?" I gasped, my head falling back against the tree, my heart pounding. "What happened?"

"He decided he had to shovel the driveway—"

"What?! But I hired someone to come and do that—"

Cold infiltrated the airwaves. "Except that *someone* didn't show up and your father decided he couldn't wait for me to come over and do it."

So many things wrong with that statement.

Why the company I'd hired hadn't shown up, why Aaron would still be seeing my father, why my father would think it was a good idea to go out and shovel his driveway at sixty-nine years old after surviving four heart attacks.

"Is he okay?"

"He needs surgery."

I gasped. "Oh my God! I—"

Cheers erupted from the audience behind me, Damon and Eden probably making their way down the aisle.

"Never mind. I can tell you're busy. I shouldn't have called," Aaron said, still cold, still so similar to how he'd sounded when I'd told him I was leaving—moving to L.A., leaving Utah behind. So different from how he'd sounded when we'd been together. But I'd made his warmth disappear as easily as freshly baked pumpkin pie around my father.

My father.

Shit.

Eyes burning at the thought of him all alone in the hospital. "I'll be on—"

Another cheer, voices coming my way.

"Enjoy your party, Mags."

I'd been about to say I'd be on the next plane home, but Aaron hung up.

And I was left with silence in my ear, a worried and aching heart . . . alone but somehow still surrounded by people.

Alone, but not.

That was fitting.

Sighing, I shoved my phone into my pocket, went to retrieve my coat and purse, bypassing the bride and groom, not wanting to spoil their special day. Then I called a Lyft, headed to the airport, and hopped on the first plane to Utah.

To Aaron—

No. To my father.

Only my father. Because Aaron was strictly in the past. We were over. There wasn't a future for us.

I'd made certain of it.

But as the plane soared across the sky, closing the distance between present and past, I was having a hard time remembering *why* I'd made certain of it.

I missed him.

And I'd . . . never stopped loving him.

END SCENE

MAGGIE AND AARON'S STORY IS COMING AUGUST
24TH, 2020

Preorder at www.books2read.com/EndScene

LOVE, CAMERA, ACTION

Dotted Line

Action Shot

Close Up

End Scene

LOVE, CAMERA, ACTION

Did you miss any of the other Love, Camera, Action series books? Check out excerpts from the series below or find the full series at http://elisefaber.com/LoveCameraAction

Dotted Line
Love, Camera, Action #1
Get your copy at books2read.com/DottedLine

Olivia

THE COLD VOICE hit my spine before I made it to my chair.

"What did you say?"

Cole McTavish.

A tall hunk of a former hockey player, all muscled thighs and towering height, with a face that would have been classified as beautiful if not for the several-times-broken nose, the jagged scar along his jaw, and the small, smooth one bisecting his left eyebrow.

Further that, he was about as opposite from me as anyone I'd ever met.

Relaxed, always ready with an easy smile, Cole never raised his voice—at least *off* the ice. On it, he'd been a terror, a virtually unstoppable force who'd fought when needed and didn't back down from protecting a teammate.

I'd also been his agent while he was playing.

After he'd retired, I'd transitioned him over to Devon, who'd helped him refine his brand for post-playing opportunities. Now, he was the face for a few hockey companies and one well-known corporation that sold watches. Though, to my and the rest of the female populace's dismay, he'd turned down the swimwear ads.

I'd been with him in the locker room enough to know what was under those flannel shirts and jeans.

It was definitely billboard worthy.

Lane started to push by him, but Cole grabbed his shoulder and stepped into my office, forcing Lane back.

Devon Scott trailed them in, a stormy expression on his face.

I glanced at my boss and shook my head, silently telling him I'd already handled it, but Dev shook his head firmly back at me. Which was when I realized that what Lane had said must have been worse than I'd thought. Normally, Devon would never get involved in an argument between my employees and myself unless I asked him to.

Which I didn't.

Since I handled my own shit.

"Tell her what you said."

My gaze flashed to Cole and his darkened face. "It's—"

Emerald eyes locked onto mine, sparking fire. "Tell her," he said, and Lane must have realized exactly how deep of a pile of shit he'd dived into because when I broke Cole's stare to glance at my assistant, his face had gone pale.

I rested my hip against my desk. "I don't need to hear it. Lane, get the file."

Devon crossed his arms. "Tell her," he said. "If you're man enough to mutter it under your breath, you're man enough to say it aloud."

Lane shook off Cole and spun to face me. "Fine," he snapped. "I said that you're such a fucking bitch."

My lips curved and I huffed. "Okay, great, thanks. Now, back to work."

Lane's jaw fell open.

A curl of amusement crept onto Dev's face.

Cole appeared even more infuriated.

Lane somehow went paler. "Wh-what?"

"I've got a ton of work," I told him, "and you say bitch like it's a bad thing." I transferred my gaze to Cole and Dev. "*All* of you are acting like it's the worst insult in the world." I laughed. "Believe me, I've been called worse."

"It's unacceptable," Dev said, and I loved the guy for it.

But this was also the way of the world.

Most men despised strong women. We were told to smile or look happy or be fine with the scraps they tossed our way. If I'd had an issue with men calling me a bitch, I would have quit this male-dominated field ten years ago when I'd been a lowly assistant like Lane and my boss had been a lot worse than a bitch.

But I hadn't.

I'd put my head down, got my shit done.

And I'd learned to not give two craps when a man thought I was a bitch.

Because it had become my anthem.

When I negotiated my client to have equivalent perks in their contract, I was a bitch.

When I demanded a different client have access to the same off-season training as the rest of the team, I was a bitch.

When I secured a bonus that was similar to the rest of the big names on the roster, I was a bitch.

So, fine.

I was a bitch.

Great. Congrats. Moving on.

—Get your copy at www.books2read.com/DottedLine

Action Shot

Love, Camera, Action #2

Get your copy at books2read.com/ActionShot

"You're Artie." Pierce Daniels, the aforementioned handsome, young director, answered his own question and sat in the chair opposite me.

It was late-afternoon in L.A., the restaurant we were in was one of my favorites, and I'd become fancy and important enough—*ha*—that they'd let me come in before they opened. Fancy and important had its perks, though this particular perk was mostly because I liked the chef—female, insanely good with all things carb-related (which was a feat sometimes in the land of Hollywood), and driven—and so I'd become a silent partner in the restaurant.

"I'm Artie," I confirmed. "Nice to meet you, Pierce."

He pulled out a laptop and I laughed internally. God, I loved energetic new blood, loved he was so excited about this project that he'd brought materials to go over. I'd been in the industry long enough to be jaded and cynical.

Pierce had exactly the kind of enthusiasm we needed in this town.

"Thanks for meeting with me," he said, powering up the computer. "I loved *In For a Penny*"—the first film I'd produced that had made its way to the awards circuit and also had garnered me my first Oscar—"but I think my favorite is actually *Into the Fire*."

I smiled. "Thanks for saying that." I set my glass on the table. "I was able to screen your most recent film. It's going to be a hit."

Notice I didn't subscribe to false flattery.

Objectively, I didn't like his movies.

However, that didn't mean I was immune to the knowledge that he was supremely talented.

He froze for a minute, studying me closely, and I was locked in place by a pair of the prettiest eyes I'd ever seen. Stormy gray with indigo bisecting their depths. Those irises darkened, understanding clouding his expression.

Click.

The laptop shut.

"It's a no," he announced, sitting back in his chair almost haphazardly.

I frowned.

"You're a no on the film."

My fingers circled the stem of my water glass. "It's a no," I agreed. "Probably the stupidest no I'll ever give, considering how successful you'll be in the next year or two." I lifted the cup to my lips, took a sip. "But the script just isn't something I'll ever make."

A lock of brown hair drifted over his forehead, giving the twenty-something-year-old director the appearance of someone even younger.

He brushed it back, almost annoyingly.

"Why not?" he asked. "The female lead is strong, more

powerful than most of the men in the film, and that dynamic is something you specialize in."

Cute.

"Yes, she *is* strong." I waited a beat. "However, that strength is undermined by a theme of the male co-star saving the day every step of the way. I counted at least three fight scenes where she's nearly beaten before the hero sweeps in to rescue her, not to mention his masterful ability to always get her naked and the snarky comments he makes about her driving skills."

Pierce was quiet for a long time. Then he nodded. "You're right."

The waiter came over and set a plate in front of me then handed a menu to Pierce. He took it, ordering an iced tea.

"You don't have to stay, if you don't want," I told him. "But if you do, I'll still buy you lunch."

His brows pulled down. "I thought I was buying *you* lunch."

A shake of my head. "I usually pay if I'm delivering disappointing news."

He laughed. "Ah. The stories of you are true."

I'd been busily spearing a forkful of handmade pasta, readying to shove it in my mouth, when he spoke. "What the hell does that mean?" I asked, after chewing and swallowing.

"Just that everyone says you're the most honest person in Hollywood."

Shrugging, I stuck the fork in my mouth and moaned when the delicious brown butter sauce made every single one of my taste buds orgasm. "It's true," I agreed.

He tilted his head to the side, considering. "So, what did you think of *Sunday Night*?"

"Hated it."

He burst into laughter and set the menu on the table, gesturing to the waiter. "I'll have what she's having." The waiter nodded and Pierce turned back to face me. "How about *Blue*?

"Nope. Didn't like it."

One brown brow rose. "Well, it's better than hate, so I'll take it. Though, I'm almost afraid to ask what you think of *Life and—*"

"Worst one of the bunch."

More laughter as he grabbed his laptop off the table and stuck it into his backpack. "I do love an honest woman."

It was my turn to lift a brow. "What's that right there?" I waved my hand at his chest. "What's going on with all of that?"

"With what?" he asked innocently.

"This smolder nonsense you have going on."

His lips twitched. "Smolder?"

"Don't tell me you're one of those guys who's too good for Disney movies," I said and shoved another bite into my mouth. "*Tangled* is the best of the bunch."

"That's the crazy talking," he countered. "Clearly *The Emperor's New Groove* is better."

I gasped. "Them's fighting words, Pierce Daniels." But my lips twitched. "Pull the lever?" I asked innocently, quoting one of my favorite lines from the film.

Heat flickered in his eyes and head leaned forward. "Wrong lever?"

I laughed. "Okay, so maybe you do have some Disney street cred."

"Actually," he said, leaning back slightly to allow the waiter to set the plate in front of him. "I think those two things are actually mutually exclusive." A beat. "But thanks for appreciating it. Even *if* that's the only thing you appreciate about me."

"That is true," I teased, shoving a bite of pasta into my mouth and barely able to hold back my moan of pleasure.

Pierce gave me an affronted look, but then he picked up a forkful of food and stuck it in his mouth.

I waited.

His eyes widened in surprise.

I knew the feeling because I'd experienced it just over a year ago, when I'd first tasted the chef's food. Hence, my being a silent partner in a risky investment. Still, good food was half the battle and I'd eaten here enough to know that the other important part—service—was also exceptional.

But Pierce didn't know that.

"This is delicious," he said around the bite, which meant it sounded a lot like "Shish sish shulishush."

"Is this where I say chew with your mouth closed before surrendering to the smolder?"

He wiped his mouth with a napkin, set down the fork. "This is where I say I don't give two shits about anything besides the amazing food on my plate." He dropped the napkin back into his lap. "How did you find this place?"

I shrugged. "A lady doesn't give away her secrets."

Stormy gray-blue eyes went hot. "I bet I can convince you."

My pussy clenched. Straight up, right then. With a single look. *Uh-oh.* "I don't date children."

He laughed. "I'm twenty-two. That's hardly a child."

"Pierce. I'm thirty-seven."

"So?"

He meant it, too, I could tell.

"So, I don't date people who work with me."

His laughter burned a hole straight down to my middle. "I think we've quite established the fact that we're not going to be working together."

He had a point. And the stink knew it, given the way those hot eyes traced me up and down.

"Eat your pasta," he ordered huskily. Normally orders from men pissed me off, especially men who were many years younger than me, who deigned to think they had a right to give me orders, but there was something about Pierce's gaze, heavy with approval and desire, that made it less annoying and more . . . promising.

I lifted a brow. "And if I don't?"

"I'll just have to—" He broke off and waggled his brows, making like he was going to grab my plate.

I lifted my fork threateningly.

He laughed, went back to his own entrée. "Thanks for lunch."

My carefully constructed bite of pasta fell onto my plate. "I thought we'd established *you* were paying," I said and when he did nothing more but chuckle and then smolder at me again, before continuing to devour his lunch, I knew I was in trouble.

Then deep shit when he snagged the waiter and handed him his card.

And then falling down into a crevice of even deeper shit when he gently tugged my ponytail out from underneath the collar of my jacket when I slipped it on.

Between the table and front door, I considered my options.

At the front door, I made a decision.

I took his hand and pulled him over to my car.

—Get your copy at www.books2read.com/ActionShot

End Scene
Love, Camera, Action #4
www.books2read.com/EndScene
Coming August 24th, 2020

ALSO BY ELISE FABER

Billionaire's Club (**all stand alone**)

Bad Night Stand

Bad Breakup

Bad Husband

Bad Hookup

Bad Divorce

Bad Fiancé

Bad Boyfriend

Bad Blind Date

Bad Wedding (July 19th, 2020)

Bad Engagement (October 12th, 2020)

Chauvinist Stories (**all stand alone**)

Bitch

Cougar

Whore

End Scene

Love After Midnight (**all stand alone**)

Rum and Notes

Virgin Daiquiri (June 29th, 2020)

Gold Hockey (**all stand alone**)

Blocked

Backhand

Boarding

Benched

Breakaway

Breakout

Checked

Coasting (June 15th, 2020)

Life Sucks Series (**all stand alone**)

Train Wreck

Hot Mess (coming soon)

Roosevelt Ranch Series (**all stand alone, series complete**)

Disaster at Roosevelt Ranch

Heartbreak at Roosevelt Ranch

Collision at Roosevelt Ranch

Regret at Roosevelt Ranch

Desire at Roosevelt Ranch

Phoenix Series (**read in order**)

Phoenix Rising

Dark Phoenix

Phoenix Freed

Phoenix: LexTal Chronicles (**rereleasing soon, stand alone, Phoenix world**)

From Ashes

In Flames

To Smoke

KTS Series

Fire and Ice (Hurt Anthology, stand alone)

Stand Alones

Someday, Maybe (YA)

ABOUT THE AUTHOR

USA Today bestselling author, Elise Faber, loves chocolate, Star Wars, Harry Potter, and hockey (the order depending on the day and how well her team -- the Sharks! -- are playing). She and her husband also play as much hockey as they can squeeze into their schedules, so much so that their typical date night is spent on the ice. Elise changes her hair color more often than some people change their socks, loves sparkly things, and is the mom to two exuberant boys. She lives in Northern California. Connect with her in her Facebook group, the Fabinators or find more information about her books at www.elisefaber.com.

facebook.com/elisefaberauthor

amazon.com/author/elisefaber

bookbub.com/profile/elise-faber

instagram.com/elisefaber

goodreads.com/elisefaber

pinterest.com/elisefaberwrite

www.ingramcontent.com/pod-product-compliance
Lightning Source LLC
Chambersburg PA
CBHW022150240626
47153CB00007B/2603